Puffin Books
The Friends

'Monkey-chaser' and 'teacher's pet' - that's what the children in her new school call Phyllisia . . They don't like her because she's an outsider. She comes from the West Indies, speaks with a different accent, and can answer more questions in class. The only person who'd like to be her friend is the untidy, cheeky, irrepressible Edith – but Phyllisia doesn't *want* to make friends with such a ragamuffin. Then comes the dreadful day when she gets beaten up in a fight after school. And when, the next morning, Edith stands forward as her protector, their friendship at last gets under way.

Life still goes on being troublesome for Phyllisia. Her domineering father, her mother, loving but sometimes strangely distant, and her sister, so much prettier and more successful than herself, all mean problems. And though she gets a lot of fun out of Edith's company, she still has some qualms about being friends with a girl who lives in a slum. It isn't until she and Edith both have to face real tragedy that Phyllisia comes to understand the value of true friendship.

This powerful book tells of a way of life that will be unfamiliar to many readers – but everyone who's had a friend will recognize themselves in it, and probably find something to learn, as well.

Rosa Guy

The Friends

Puffin Books
in association with Victor Gollancz Ltd

Puffin Books, Penguin Books Ltd, Harmondsworth, Middlesex, England
Viking Penguin Inc., 40 West 23rd Street, New York, New York 10010, U.S.A.
Penguin Books Australia Ltd, Ringwood, Victoria, Australia
Penguin Books Canada Ltd, 2801 John Street, Markham, Ontario, Canada L3R 1B4
Penguin Books (N.Z.) Ltd, 182–190 Wairau Road, Auckland 10, New Zealand

First published in Great Britain by Victor Gollancz 1974
Published in Puffin Books 1977
Reprinted 1980, 1981, 1983, 1984, 1985

Made and printed in Great Britain by
Hazell Watson & Viney Limited,
Member of the BPCC Group,
Aylesbury, Bucks
Set in Monotype Times

To those who love,
to those who want to love,
and to Walter

Part One

1

Her name was Edith.

I did not like her. Edith always came to school with her clothes unpressed, her stockings bagging about her legs with big holes, which she tried to hide by pulling them into her shoes but which kept slipping up, on each heel, to expose a round, brown circle of dry skin the size of a quarter. Of course there were many children in this class that were untidy and whom I did not like. Some were tough. So tough that I was afraid of them. But at least they did not have to sit right across the aisle from me. Nor did they try to be friendly as Edith did – whenever she happened to come to school.

Edith walked into the classroom at late morning, causing the teacher to stop in the middle of one of her monotonous sentences to fasten a hate-filled glare, which Edith never saw, on her back.

'Good afternoon, Miss Jackson,' the teacher's voice, thick with sarcasm, followed her to her seat. But Edith, popping bubble gum on her back teeth so that it distorted her square little face, slammed her books on the desk, slipped her wiry body into her seat, then turned her head around the room nodding greetings to friends.

The teacher's voice rose sharply: 'It seems to me that if you *had* to honour us with your presence today, you could at least have been preparing yourself to come to class looking presentable.'

Her words had more effect on the class than on Edith. They always did. When I had first come into class I had thought it was because the teacher was white. Later I realized that it was because of the manner she spoke to the pupils. Now, the shuffle of feet sounded around the room, a banging of desks. The teacher shrilled: 'I am talking to you, Edith Jackson.'

'Huh, what? – oh, you talking to me? Good afternoon, Miss Lass.' Edith grinned with open-faced innocence. The teacher reddened. Edith turned her impish grin to include all of the appreciative snickers around the room. She then leaned across the aisle and said to me: 'Hi ya doin', Phyllisia?'

I pulled myself tall in my seat, made haughty little movements with my shoulders and head, adjusted the frills on the collar of my well-ironed blouse, touched my soft, neatly plaited hair and pointedly gave my attention to the blackboard.

Edith ignored my snub. She always ignored my snubs. Edith had made up her mind, from the first day I entered this class, that she would be my friend whether I wanted it or not. 'Ain't it a pretty day out?' She grinned and made a loud explosion with her gum. 'Sure hated to come and stick myself in this dingy-ass classroom.'

Her words pulled my attention away from the blackboard and to the window where the sun came splashing into the room.

Since my father had sent for us, my sister Ruby who is sixteen and me, two years younger, and set us down in

10

this miserable place called Harlem, New York, this was the first warm day. I, too, had not wanted to come here today. Walking to school, seeing people coming out of their homes with faces softened by smiles, for the first time I had been filled with the desire to run off somewhere, anywhere but to this room. I had not wanted to have to listen to a teacher I did not like, nor to sit among children I liked even less. But where could I go? I knew nothing about this strange city. Going one block out of my way between home and school, and I would be lost. And so I had come, grudgingly, but I had come.

Yet the moment I had entered the classroom, I knew that my instincts had been right. I should not have come today. The same recklessness that had pulled at me in the streets was big in the room, pulling and tugging at the control of the students. Fear cut a zigzag pattern from my stomach to my chest: The students in the class did not like *me*.

They mocked my West Indian accent, called me names – 'monkey' was one of the nicer ones. Sometimes they waited after school to tease me, following me at times for several blocks, shouting. But it had been cold and after a time they had been only too glad to hunch their shoulders up to their ears and go home. Winter, as much as I hated it, had protected me. Now it was spring.

Automatically my gaze sought the big-breasted girl sitting diagonally across the room from me – Beulah. Beulah sat with her head bowed down to the desk obviously reading a comic book she had concealed beneath. Beulah was the toughest girl I had ever known. She was so tough that she did anything she wanted to in class, and Miss Lass looked the other way. But the worst of it was that Beulah for some reason *hated* me.

'Come on, let's split this scene,' Edith whispered. 'I got money. We can go to some jazzy place and wait the time out.'

Her words lit my mind with pictures of what she meant by jazzy places – places like parks and lakes and outdoor movies. All I had to do was turn and smile at this dirty little girl and she could take me to places that I had never been to before. But then I thought about Calvin and the brilliant thoughts fizzled out.

Calvin is my father. To myself I use his first name, as a sign of disrespect. The first week we had come, I demanded of him why he had sent for us to set us down in this trap of asphalt and stone called Harlem. 'Because I have the right. To control your rudeness better,' he had said. 'What blame control does he think we need,' I had muttered to my sister Ruby loud enough for him to hear. The next moment my lips were swelling up from a backhand slap. I had not even seen it coming. '*Who* needs control?' he asked. I sulked at first, refusing to answer. But the next time he said, 'I ask you, who needs control?' I gave one look into his set, black face, with anger burning out of his eyes, and my determination not to answer flickered out. 'Me,' I answered meekly, and my hatred of him mounted.

No, it would not do for Calvin to see me out in the streets when I should be in school. And with someone looking like Edith?

I pulled my attention back into the room just in time to hear Miss Lass throw a question in my direction.

'Can anyone tell me on what continent the country of Egypt is located?' she asked.

I stared fixedly at the blackboard. While it was certain I could not leave school, it was also certain that I did not feel like standing in the full glare of the children's animosity on this warm touchy day to answer any questions.

Teacher waited. The class waited. I waited, praying someone else would know the answer and, barring that, Miss Lass herself would explain. I did not remember her ever discussing Africa before. But I had been the star pupil too long – always jumping up to let others know how smart I was. And so Miss Lass kept looking at me while I kept looking at the blackboard. Finally, after a few minutes, she called: 'Phyllisia?'

I did not move. Why did she want to make an example of me to the other children? There were at least thirty others she could call on. 'Phyllisia!' I still kept my seat. I kept repeating to myself: I will not stand. I will not answer. I will not.

Then someone snickered, and someone else. My face burned with shame. Sitting there and not answering was like begging. And why should I beg? I had done nothing to anybody. I found myself standing. I heard my voice saying, despite a sixth sense warning me to remain silent, to stay in my seat, 'Egypt is in Africa.' Once started I kept on talking to dispel any notion that I might be guessing. 'It is bordered on the South by the Sudan and on the North by the Mediterranean Sea which opens up into the Nile, which is the longest river in Africa and perhaps the world.'

I resumed my seat, a taste of chalk in my mouth, unsatisfied with the display of my brilliance. Nor did I feel any better at the flurry of shuffling feet, the banging of more desks and the sound of contemptuous whispers.

'No it ain't either,' a boy shouted from the back of the room. 'They got A-rabs in Egypt. Everybody know ain't no A-rabs in Africa.'

'That's where you are wrong,' Miss Lass shrilled. 'Egypt *is* a country in Africa. If some of you would follow Phyllisia's example and study your books, then perhaps the intelligence rate in this room might zoom up to zero.'

Silently I groaned. Miss Lass had to know better. She had to know that she was setting me up as a target. Any fool would feel the agitation in the room. But that was exactly what she wanted!

I knew it suddenly. Standing in front of the room, her blonde hair pulled back to emphasize the determination of her face, her body girdled to emphasize the determination of her spine, her eyes holding determinedly to anger, *Miss Lass was afraid!!* She was afraid and she was using *me* to keep the hatred of the children away from *her*. I was the natural choice because I was a stranger and because I was proud.

The thought seemed to be so loud that it drew her attention, and for one moment we stared startled into each other's eyes. Her face turned a beet red and she shifted her gaze.

I felt a dozen needles sticking in my stomach. I leaned back in my seat. The fingernails of the girl behind me dug into my back. 'Teacher's pet,' she hissed. I pulled away, but as I did my head magnetically turned and I found myself staring into the eyes of the thick-muscled girl with the breasts. She had turned completely around in her seat so that her back faced the teacher while she stared at me. As our stares locked, she balled

14

up her fist, put it first over one eye and then the other. The needles in my stomach multiplied by thousands.

But Edith, unaware of anything unnatural happening, leaned across the aisle, her eyes wide with admiration. 'Girl, you sure are smart. I bet ain't nothing your folks don't teach you, 'cause you sure ain't learned them things in here.'

Relieved to break the belligerent stare, I turned, but remembered *who* had spoken, in time to check my gratitude with a stiff nod. Still my heart was thumping. I had to keep telling myself that it was, after all, only the first period. By the end of the day things had to settle back to normal. So I waited anxiously for the bell to signal the end of the period and the change of class.

2

By the last period what had started out as a mild spring day flourished into full summer heat. The children, shouting and screaming, came charging back into their homeroom. The discipline established during winter at the expense of the teacher's good disposition had been washed away by the sudden warmth. It took the last bit of Miss Lass's energy to maintain shoestring control as we waited for the final bell.

I did not want the bell to ring. All of the pupils' restlessness, their resentment over their senseless imprisonment on this overripe day, seemed directed towards me, as well as the serpentine stare that big-breasted Beulah kept burning at the side of my face. I did not want to leave the classroom. Tempted to ask Miss Lass to let me stay to help with chores after school, I changed my mind at the look of her face shiny from sweat, with its lips gone along with her lipstick, the escaped strands of blonde hair hanging limply over her angular face – her look of aching wickedness.

I had waited for Edith.

Edith had not come in with the rest of the class. She never did. Teacher called her a straggler. Today when she straggled in from her last class I intended to surprise her. I was going to smile and make friends with her. At one time during the day I had reasoned that the children singled me out for abuse because I walked alone. They might leave me in peace if I walked with a friend. And so I had sat staring at the door waiting for the one girl I could use, my heart giving little leaps of delight everytime someone entered, and sinking in dismay – almost down to my stomach – when it was not Edith.

Soon, however, I had accepted the obvious. Edith had carried out her earlier promise and had ducked out of school as the weather grew warmer. Now I wanted to leave too, panicky at the feeling of violence around me. If I were just to get up and go, start running, I could be far away from the school before class was dismissed. But gathering enough courage to simply walk out was not easy, and between the thought and the moment to act the bell rang, and the class made their dash for freedom.

A crowd was waiting for me when I walked down the outside steps of the school. They had gathered as though the entire school had been given notice that a rumble was on. Leaving no doubt that I was the intended victim, a bloody roar rose when I appeared on the steps.

Glancing through the crowd with pretended casualness, I picked out some of my classmates. Most were standing in front, with big-breasted Beulah first, her evil intentions plastered over her face. The thin girl who had dug her fingernails in my back stood behind her, whispering excitedly in her ear.

On stoops around the school and across the street, grownups stood looking at the yelling mob. At windows of buildings more adults adjusted themselves to get a better view. Was there one who might come down to help a young girl, desperate with fear, ready to be set upon by a mob? I knew the answer. No.

My pride was crumbling. To preserve some of it, I had to move quickly. So, holding my book bag tightly to my chest, I stuck my head up, walked down the steps and pushed boldly past Beulah, with her big breasts pushed aggressively out.

But my back quivered as I passed as though it had eyes and actually did see the powerful hands reach out and push me. Push me towards a little boy who stepped cunningly out of my way. And there I was face to face with the girl who sat behind me in class.

This girl was tall and as thin as I. I knew I could match her strength. But what if I started to fight her and Beulah jumped in too? While trying to make up my mind, the thin girl quickly shoved me back into the waiting leathery arms of the girl I feared the most.

'You dirty West Indian,' she hissed in my ear. 'You ain't rapping so big out here, is you? No, you ain't rapping so big out here. We should get Miss Lassy-assy out so she can see how you ain't doing no big-time talking and acting better than anybody.'

'West Indian?' A boy called out. 'My Ma call them monkey chasers.'

'Monkey chaser, monkey chaser, bring monkey soup for your monkey father.'

Someone else shouted in a mock West Indian accent: 'Run her into the sea, mahn. What she want here nohow? We ain't got no trees to swing from.'

My dry tongue licked drier lips, my knees buckled as I tried once again to push through the dense crowd. Blocking my way was a boy who stuck his hand under my chin. 'Best man hit this.' It was their idea of fair play: If I was a 'good sport', I would hit the boy's hand,

18

the boy would then hit Beulah, who would complete the cycle by hitting me to start the fight.

I pretended I did not see the hand.

'West Indian ain't gonna hit shit,' Beulah sneered. 'I'll hit it.' She hit the hand. The hand in turn hit me. I was now supposed to hit Beulah to complete the cycle. My body quaked. I clutched my book bag to my chest and again tried to shoulder my way through.

'Pardon me,' I said, forcing polite-ness. 'I . . .'

'Dig that rap,' the thin girl jeered. 'Pardon me. Who the hell she think she is?'

'Always trying to act better than the folks,' Beulah sneered. Then with her thick, strong hands she spun me around punching her fist against my nose. 'Don't push me,' she yelled at the same time. 'You see she pushed me?' Not expecting any answer she kept on punching and punching.

Blood ran from my nose and I tasted more in my mouth. I encircled my head with my arms. A blow caught me in my ribs. I doubled over, put my book bag to protect my stomach, and the fists pounded my face again.

'Old Big-Tits sure can fight.'

'Yeah. She gonna smash that monkey into a African monkey stew.'

I crouched trying to arouse pity. If not in the children, certainly in some of the grownups looking on. That was a mistake. At my look of utter helplessness the children jeered. 'Let's finish her off,' someone yelled. They moved in around me.

In terror I levelled my head, rammed it in the direction of the jabbing fists. It contacted with the fleshy chest. The girl staggered. I backed up, rammed forward again. This time the thick, tough girl sprawled backwards to the sidewalk and lay there squirming in pain. I ran over her, kicked her face out of the way of my flying feet, hit the person in front of me with my shoulder – the crowd opened up and I ran for my life.

I did not feel the ground beneath my feet nor see the street crossings. I heard horns blowing, brakes screeching, blending with the jeers which seemed a very part of the air that I was so painfully breathing. Clouds of fear came and went carrying me for blocks before I realized that no one was following me. By that time, exhausted, unable to run further, I leaned against the iron rail of an apartment building, holding my sides and gasping for breath.

'Oh God, I hate those kids,' I muttered. 'I hate them. I hate them.' Tears came, and I wiped them from my eyes and the blood from my nose with one sweep of my arm. I examined my face with my fingers, touched my thickened lips, the swelling that stretched my skin smooth, hiding the dividing lines that separated nose from cheeks, then tears came again.

Walking slowly, painfully towards my street, I stared hard into the faces of grownups, searching for a look of pity, of concern, wishing just one person to ask me: 'What happened, little girl?' Then I could explain to somebody, and they might tell me what I was doing wrong. Why nobody liked me. But no older person stopped to look at me or to ask me. They just did not notice me.

Children were chasing one another over someone's furniture set out on the sidewalk. They rode up and down on the sofa and the springs of the bed. Up and down, up and down. The adult world simply walked by.

Things were so different at home. On The Island everybody cared about everything. Grownups would never let a bunch of children fight only one. They would break up the fight and chase them all away. Nor would they let children walk on top of people's furniture; they would stop them and scold them and send them on their way.

But then, at home, fourteen-year-old girls did not fight. We had other things to do. We rushed home from school to take off our shoes and to play with the cooling earth through our toes. Or sometimes we would help the boys steal fruits from the neighbours' trees. And there, nothing was wrong about being alone either.

I remembered how much I used to like being alone. At times, instead of going home from school, I used to go into the bush to listen to pretty little birds quarrel in their harsh voices. I used to walk around the village, and climbing the highest hill I lay looking down at people moving beneath me like so many insects. I would forget time as I let my gaze play around the green of the trees, the bright reds of fruits, the pale blues and pinks of flowers, while the wind wove everything into different patterns from one minute to the next.

But being alone *here* meant being abused and threatened and beaten up.

My legs ached as I walked. My body felt heavy with its load of bruises, and my thoughts kept going back to the girl I had butted and left squirming on the ground. What will happen tomorrow? Tomorrow she might not give me the chance to butt her. She might be waiting for me early in the morning, with her hard strong fists ready to finish off what she had started today.

'I'm not going back to that school. I don't care what anyone says. I'm not going back,' I muttered loudly, glaring around at the adult world as though every one of them – grouping together, laughing together, talking together as they enjoyed the warm day – was responsible for my pain.

But I was sure that when Mother saw how badly they had done me, she would not send me back. It was Calvin, of course, who would force me to go. But I wasn't going. Anyway I hated Calvin. I hated him just as I hated the children and the school and the teacher. 'I don't care what he says. I'm not going back. Even if he beats me, I'm not going back.'

Then I looked up the block. Suddenly I realized that my hat was twisted on my head. I felt the fluff of lace collar sticking out of my coat, tickling my chin. I became miserably aware that the front and sleeves of my coat were covered with blood, and I knew that my stockings had fallen about my shoes exposing my thin legs.

With a sudden burst of energy I sprinted up the street, dashed into my building, and racing up the stairs two at a time flew into the apartment. Coming down the street, towering over everyone, like some giant in a fairy story, gesticulating with his hands and arms and shoulders as he talked, showing off his well-tailored grey suit with its diamond tiepin glittering in the sun, strode Calvin.

3

Rushing into the apartment, planning to hide in my room, I ran right into my mother's arms. '*Bon Dieu*,' she cried after one look at my face. 'What is this? What have they done to you?'

The look of my mother – tall, and an olive complexion with black, black eyes – has always awed me. As I saw her now, heard her voice, rich, deep, softened by the French Creole of The Island – it tickled the pores of my skin, thickened my throat with unshed tears and jumbled my words as they fell thick and heavy from my swollen lips.

'Al – all the chi – child – ren bunch up and wa – ant to fi – fight me.'

'Want to? From the look of your face I would say they did fight you.' She called to my sister. 'Ruby, Ruby, bring me a basin of water and a rag.' Then pulling me into the living room, she sat on the couch holding me to her knees. 'Tell me, Phyllisia, why? Don't the children like you?'

The pity in her voice pushed me to the brink of hysterics. 'No. They hate me! Everybody hates me!'

'But how so?'

'I an – swer the que – questions the teach – er asks and – and the gi – girl be – hind says that I – I'm teacher's pet. And wh – hen I co – me down – stairs th – they all stand around wait – ing . . .'

'How long has this been going on?'

'Si – ince the be – begin – ning. They say all ki – kinds of nas – ty things to – to me.'

'Nasty things like what?'

'They – they call me mon – monkey chaser.'

Ruby had come into the room with the basin of water. Mother turned to her: 'Do you have trouble like this, Ruby?'

'No, Mother.'

'Why is that? Is it because the children are older in your school?'

'It is because I don't stick my hand in the air all the time and try to prove how smart I am.' Ruby spoke in her usual, vain, airy manner. 'After all, Mother, you know how Phyllisia is. If she did not try to act so smart and know-it-all, she would not be opening up her mouth and continually be reminding the children where she comes from.'

All of my self-pity turned into a need for revenge. But I held myself at Mother's knees not to rush up and scratch at her pretty face.

Mother's eyes had widened. A pulse beat rapidly at her delicate throat. 'Ruby, are you standing there telling me that you do not answer questions in class because you are ashamed of where you come from?'

Ruby did not notice the reproach in Mother's voice and went on in the same manner, 'Well, the children don't like it and the teachers don't demand it, so why call attention to oneself? Sometimes when the children don't know the answer, I even slip it to them.'

Aghast, Mother cried: 'Is so? For shame, for shame, Ruby. I did not know that you were ashamed of yourself.'

24

'I am not ashamed of myself, Mother.' Ruby hated to be scolded. Tears rose quickly to her eyes. 'But I want people to like me.'

'Ruby, you are a nice-looking girl. You are well-mannered. If you can also add intelligence to that list, then you must look elsewhere for the reasons people don't like you.'

Mother's displeasure gave me new confidence. 'Mother,' I pleaded, 'I don't want to go back to that school tomorrow. Please, don't make me go back to that school.'

'You have to,' she said quietly. 'You are a West Indian girl going to school in New York and you are proud. What happens in this school will happen in any other. So if you must fight, you must.'

For a moment I just stared. Did she know what it was to have a yelling mob ready to pounce on you? Or to have someone as tough as Big-Tits hate you for nothing? And to know that she would be waiting for you the next day? I thrust my swollen face angrily near to hers. 'I don't bargain with my intelligence, but I don't want to be killed for it either.'

'Oh, they will not kill you.' I felt her withdrawing into that calm where nothing could reach her.

Usually I admired this 'haughtiness'. I often imitated it when I played the role of 'grand lady'. Now however I wanted to snatch at the calm, shock her into an anger to equal mine. How dared she sit there – inside of herself – and state that I would not be killed!

'I can't fight them all,' I shouted. 'I can't fight a bunch of ragamuffins whom I never did anything to and who hate me.'

Mother lowered her eyes to conceal her annoyance. I

had deliberately used the word ragamuffin, which Calvin used in talking about the people of Harlem when he wanted to offend her.

But she did not scold. 'They don't hate you, Phyllisia. They are probably full of resentment. And who would not be resentful in a city so tense, so oppressive as New York? But they don't hate you.'

Stifling the urge to throw myself on the floor, to kick, to scream, have a tantrum, I screeched instead, 'But it's me they're fighting!'

She smiled condescendingly. 'You *are* a smart girl, Phyllisia, so try to understand. The children pick on you because you are still strange to them. But this time will pass. You wait and see. The children you are fighting today will be your friends tomorrow.'

'I don't want to be their friend,' I shrieked. 'Never, never, do you hear? I don't want them to like me! I don't want to like them . . .'

'And by Christ you don't have to!' The front door had slammed and Calvin came striding into the living room. Two men walked in behind him. One I recognized as a giant of a man with whom he had been talking in the street. The other was a man much shorter, reaching Calvin only to his shoulders.

Without pausing, Calvin roared in his great voice, 'You do not have to like them nor do you have to be like them. Always keep one thing in mind, and that is, a Cathy never *have* to like or be like or act like anybody in the world besides a Cathy.'

He had been drinking. The odour of rum mixed strongly with the sweet Calvin scent of shaving lotion and tobacco. 'Now having said all of that,' he gestured eloquently to acknowledge that he had entered upon an unusual scene, 'tell me what the matter is.'

'Phyllisia had a fight at school today,' Mother explained.

He looked into my face and bellowed, 'Christ, but it must have been one bacchanal. Look at this, Charles, Frank, it is about as sweet a one as I did ever see. But don't tell me. I know it's the other girl I have to shed a tear over.'

'Sh – she was a – a big, tough girl.'

'Tough? What is that? You got a head on your shoulders. It's to use anyway you want. I always did say I'm never helpless as long as I can butt.'

'I – I did . . .'

'Eheh, chips and thing from the old block – and so?'

'Then they all bu – bunch up and want to jump me.' Tears rolled down my cheeks.

'Isso? In that case let me instruct you on what you must do. Take a brick to school in your book bag. And when you see a gang surrounding you, grab one of them. It don't matter which one. Take that brick and start beating – make sure it's her head, mind you. Just keep beating and beating until she is senseless. From that day on, mark my word,' he crossed his two index fingers and kissed them, 'all the rest will leave you alone.'

'Calvin,' Mother protested. 'You are talking about children.'

'*Mais oui*, children.' He spread his arms out. 'But she must know already to run like blazes if it is a grown man troubling her. I am *talking* about children.'

'One thing you must consider,' the shorter man stepped forward and with his handkerchief patted the tears from my puffed-up eyes. 'This little girl in question is made up of flesh and blood.'

'Now it's stupidness you talking,' Calvin exploded. 'A Cathy does not brag about the fact that he is flesh and blood. He overlooks the fact that he is flesh and blood.'

'Oh God,' the small man exclaimed. 'Before this man begins again to tell us about the invincibility of his flesh and the nobility of his blood, let me have the pleasure of introducing myself to my little family.

'Children, I am your Cousin Frank – and a Cathy too, you know? That might explain my negligence in paying my long overdue respects. That, and the fact that I am one of those Cathys who lacking nobility have to work ignoble hours to make a living.'

He wore a cigar in a smile at the corner of his mouth, and the rest of his smooth, brown face stretched out with good nature. I liked him.

'*Mon vieux*,' Mother smiled. 'But it did take you long. The children have been here for over five months already. I got to imagine that my favourite cousin had ceased to be.'

The other man frightened me. He was big. So big that the sleeves of his jacket stopped far above his wrists, leaving part of his large, bony arms and wrists naked – looking like the roots of a fallen tree. His face, too, was unnaturally big. It had harsh lines forming vales along the sides of his nose down to his chin. But then he spoke. His voice, soft and surprisingly high, almost like the voice of a woman, wiped out any idea of cruelty. He smiled and his big dark-brown face crumbled into gentleness.

'And did you think that this devoted friend had also

ceased to be, Ramona? If I did give you that impression for truth it would be true. For guilty indeed I would be to leave you to struggle alone against the greatness of Calvin's flesh. Although, I did always say, you *are* a remarkable woman to be able to bear the burden of so much greatness.'

His strange manner of phrasing, his gentle approach did more than compliment her beauty. It forced consideration of the fragility that lay just beneath her surface appearance. It reminded me that I had been shouting at her a moment before. I was ashamed.

'Not so remarkable, Charles,' Mother laughed. 'It took me a lifetime to learn.'

'One has to be able to believe a thing before one can learn,' Cousin Frank teased, the smile around his cigar deepening.

'But you always was a good one with the jokes,' Calvin said, 'What is a lifetime to you is not a lifetime to Ramona, you know? One day she raised her eyes so.' Calvin looked a short distance over his head. 'She see me. She looked down so.' He looked down at the floor. 'In that minute she had done live a lifetime.' He put his hands to his chest. 'She was and still is convinced that this flesh is great.'

Laughter, loud and warm from their long and intimate relationship, filled the room. 'The one thing that my cousin have that I most admire, outside of his wife,' Frank said, 'is his great modesty.' The room crackled again. In the midst of their laughter I felt myself yanked by my arm and my sore face being scratched by the roughness of wool. Calvin had caught me in his arms and was pressing my face against his chest.

'This is the baby,' he cried.

My father had never hugged me, not even after our long estrangement when he had met us at the airport. He had never laughed so loud in my presence or even joked in this room before. The shock of his arms around me, the sweet smell of him teasing my nostrils, the sound of pride in his voice made me wonder how a man who darkened a room with his anger could so brighten it with his laughter.

But it was only for an instant. The next moment I was staring at his back questioning if it had really happened. I heard his voice, still loud with laughter, saying: 'The trouble with that one, though, is she's ugly. Yes, man, even if you take away that fat eye and swollen nose, she still ugly.' The room plunged once again into gloom.

'But I'm lucky all the same,' he bragged. 'God ain't forget me.' Grabbing Ruby by her hand, he pulled her to centre floor. 'From now on when you old-talk about pretty people you bound to remember this one.'

'She is very much like her mother.' Charles beamed his gentle smile down on Ruby.

'You're an ass,' Calvin accused. 'What you mean her mother? This girl is a Cathy in the flesh.'

'No, man,' Cousin Frank replied. 'I never see a Cathy so pretty. And I must know.'

'But Frank,' Calvin insisted. 'You know my sister Violet.'

'Not only do I know Violet, but all of your other sisters and brothers, and I say that not one of them is so pretty. If that was true, I would have long married and been double family to these children.'

Radiant from their admiration, Ruby stood protesting in a high, false voice, 'Oh, Daddy, please. Stop, Daddy,' all the while smiling and acting coy. They had forgotten me. I turned my back to all of them and proudly stalked to the window where I stood looking out at boys and girls talking together on the stoop across the street.

'You are a lucky man, a very lucky man,' I heard Mr Charles say and Cousin Frank reply, still teasing, 'But give Ramona some credit, Charles. Calvin ain't do nothing.' Then Calvin's loud voice laughing, 'But the man mad. I tell you he mad.'

Staring out of the window I tried to block their detestable voices from my ears – especially Calvin's. He was so deceitful – hugging me just to show off. But although I successfully blocked the meaning of their words, their laughter warm and together kept hurting, kept me feeling sorry for myself.

I was plain and my family was good-looking. I hated to admit it but even Calvin with his big, broad handsomeness was dashing. Many times I stood at the window to watch people turn and stare when he passed. Mother, of course, was too pretty to describe. She was like some queen out of a fairy story – except that she was olive-tan, almost brown, and most queens in fairy stories were white. And their pride, Ruby – with her cherry-brown complexion and thick unmanageable hair – was a topic of conversation wherever she went. Ruby's eyebrows were so heavy and her eyelashes so thick and sooty black that everyone's attention was drawn to her light-brown eyes that looked sorrowful even when she was plotting wickedness. No one laughed at Ruby. It just was not easy to laugh at pretty people.

I was plain and tall, too tall for fourteen years, and without any shape. At home it had not mattered. On The Island my Aunt loved me. She had promised that soon my breasts would begin to develop. She had promised too that one day my nose would stand up straight on my face and look like my mother's. But up to this time none of her predictions had come true. My nose still remained undefined. My chest was still flat. The only thing constantly changing about me were my arms and legs, getting longer and skinnier with the years.

Everyone laughed at me. Everyone – except that girl Edith. I gazed longingly at the girls playing downstairs. If I went to play with them they would all simply stop to stare at me. If I opened my mouth to speak, they would hold their sides laughing. Even that one Marian.

I liked Marian. Marian was so brown and round and pretty. She combed her hair in two long long braids which she tied with satin bows. She wore the prettiest dresses to school and those thick, ribbed socks that were all the rage. Sometimes she even wore silk stockings.

Marian lived right across the street from me. The first week I had come, I wanted to walk to school with her. But she had given me a rude stare, looked me up and down, then had crossed the street to be with her other friends. I never looked at her any more – at least not so that she saw me. I didn't try to talk to her either. But I wanted to.

It was so lonely to be in this city without a friend. I thought of Edith for a moment, with the holes in her stockings and her square jaw working hard with her bubble gum. Then I pushed her out of my mind. I gazed sadly out at Marian, sighing. She probably would never talk to me in life. But I longed so much for her friendship. So very, very much.

4

'So this is the little lady who had so much trouble at school today?' Mr Charles had come to stand beside me, slipping an awkward arm around my shoulders. 'Don't let it trouble you too much. The first few months are the hardest.'

'It's what I tell her too, Charles,' Mother came to stand at my other side. 'This is a thing between children that is bound to pass.'

It seemed that they were both trying to apologize for having neglected me. But this did nothing to soothe my anger or ease my loneliness. Calvin, the one who had insulted me, still talked on, ignoring me. He had button-holed Cousin Frank in an eye-to-eye argument and was shouting: 'You think I joking when I say God don't forget me? I say he don't. He made two kinds of people and placed them on this earth . . .'

Mother and Mr Charles, showing their concern over me, were speaking earnestly. I wanted to listen to them:

Mother: 'Children can be so cruel.' But Calvin's voice, loud in the background, kept pulling at my attention. I heard Mr Charles answer: 'Unhappily yes. Children are by far the most cruel of all animals . . .' Loud in the background Calvin:

'He made a smart man and He made a fool!'

Wanting to shut Calvin out of my mind, I strained to

give my full attention to Mr Charles: '. . . animals imitate their elders . . .'

Cousin Frank, in the background: '. . . I just want to know which category He put you in, Calvin . . .'

Mr Charles: '. . . animals are checked by instinct. But children must move past instinct to reason . . .'

Calvin: '. . . but you make joke, man. You must see the money I make . . . Two years in this country I opened up my first restaurant . . .'

Mr Charles: '. . . But at her age, children are still in a state of confusion . . .'

Calvin: '. . . I'll open another and another . . .'

Charles: '. . . They five times worse than their elders . . .'

Calvin: '. . . I ain't like these damn fool black people . . .'

Mother: '. . . it is hard, but not half so bad as what is happening to Ruby . . .'

Calvin: '. . . they can't do this. They can't do that . . .'

Charles: 'What is happening . . . ?'

Calvin: '. . . I make money! Money don't make me . . .'

Mother: 'It's really frightening. I didn't know before today . . .'

Calvin: '. . . He look after the smart ones. He don't give a damn about the fool.'

Frank: 'Oh God Ramona! Tell me what you will do when this man wake up?'

Mother turned from the window. 'That is like asking what am I going to do about New York, Frank. I still have not made up my mind if it is Calvin that is like New York or New York that is like Calvin.'

'That,' Frank said, 'is a good one. I'll keep that. You hear Charles? Is it Calvin that is . . .'

'The resemblance is remarkable,' Charles said. 'They both seem made to dazzle the eye and to wear out the mind. But talking about New York, Ramona has something here that is seriously troubling her.'

'It's Ruby,' Mother explained. 'She tells me that she never talks or gives answers in class because she is worried that the children will laugh at her.'

'Aha!' Frank moved away from Calvin, his eyes lighting to the new subject. 'That is what is called the Americanization process. You start out in school with a head full of sense and when you leave, it is full of nonsense.'

'She knows her lessons well,' Mother went on. 'But she slips answers to the other children to gain their friendship.'

'That is bad,' Mr Charles admonished. 'Of course, there is nothing wrong in working out common problems with other students. But to exchange answers to problems for friendship will not earn you their respect.'

'They will end up always using you,' Cousin Frank agreed.

Again the attention had shifted to Ruby! *I* had come home badly beaten. I might be killed tomorrow. But they wanted me to understand the other children while they all worried about Ruby, Ruby, Ruby. Anger stretched the skin of my swollen face.

Ruby sat at the edge of the couch, her sorry-looking brown eyes filling with tears. Then Calvin came charging back into the spotlight. 'What?' He thrust his face up to hers. 'You! My child! A Cathy letting ragamuffins eat your brain? Never!' Ruby began crying in earnest.

But Calvin having captured the floor once again shifted his attack to hold it. 'Never in my life have I begged a man for friendship. They beg me. You see these hands?' He held his hands out. 'I fight with these hands and I work with these hands to get what I want. I'm a big man now and I'm going to get bigger . . .'

'Hold it! Hold it!' Mr Charles stretched his giant frame upwards, his hands touched the ceiling. 'Before we get into all this greatness again, let me bid you goodbye. No, no, Calvin. It ain't that I don't agree. But sometimes the company gets too big-shot for my blood. I gone!'

As the two men made ready to leave, Mother touched Charles gently on his arm. 'Before you go, Charles, tell me, what about this new doctor Annie is going to now?'

All of the lines on Mr Charles' massive face deepened. 'Haven't you been feeling well, Ramona?'

'It's just that I heard he was so great.'

'From Annie? But you know Annie, Ramona. For years I take her from one doctor to the next. They always start off great but become bums the minute they say she is well.'

'Come, Charles, Annie was never a well woman.'

'You mean she was never a normal woman. Always a little off. Tell me, what is with you?' His voice came back to its habitual gentleness.

Mother opened her mouth, but no words came. She turned quickly from them. The two men looked at Calvin. For once Calvin was at a loss for words. A sudden twitching shattered his handsome face. The room stopped breathing.

Then Mother turned her warm smile back on. Calvin recovered his lost speech, the fixed stares of the men wavered. The room breathed again.

'How come you are leaving so soon,' Calvin's voice boomed. 'I ain't even tell you about . . .'

'But keep something for the next time, nuh?' Cousin Frank dug his cigar deeper in the corner of his mouth. He looked at me and he winked. 'Hey, put some hot compresses on that face tonight. You will be good as new tomorrow. Ready to begin again.'

Wrenching my gaze from his, I turned away from them all and stared angrily back out of the window.

5

The moment I awoke the next morning all of my fears came rushing back. I decided not to open my eyes, not to get out of bed. I was not going back to that school no matter what Mother or Calvin or anybody in the whole wide world said. After all, it had to be up to me to decide if I would submit to being beaten or even killed. Pushing my foot out to feel for Ruby, I realized that she was not in the bed, so it must be almost time to get up. I squeezed my eyes shut and pulled the covers over my head.

'Hey, what do you think – going to sleep all day?' Ruby came into the room already dressed, smelling of sweet body powder. Roughly she pulled the cover back. Held it firmly in her hands. 'Come on, Mother said to get up.'

I opened my eyes and stared my hatred of the entire world at her, then reaching up tugged at the sheet in her hands. But snatching it off the bed, she balled it up and threw it across the room to the chair. 'You are not going back to sleep,' she asserted in her most womanish voice. I lay staring at her, ready to spring up and pull her down to the bed. But Mother's voice sounded up the hallway: 'Is she awake yet?' Sullenly I got out of bed to begin preparations for school.

In the kitchen I refused to answer Mother's cheerful greeting. 'The compresses did help a bit, don't you think?' That was all she cared about, the compresses and my swollen face, but not what was going to happen to me later. I sat down, picked up my spoon and splashed it down into my oatmeal. She sat across from me. I did not look at her. Instead I gazed around the kitchen at the colourful dishes in the open cupboards, the frilled cotton curtains that shut out the view of the air shaft, the squares of the heavily waxed linoleum. Reaching over finally, she touched my arm. 'I will come to school to talk to your teacher today.'

I suffered the touch of her hand in silence. What good would it do, I wanted to ask. Will you take me this morning and sit with me all day? Or will you stroll in later this afternoon while I am lying somewhere, bleeding to death?

In tight-lipped silence I walked beside Ruby on the way to our schools. I had firmly made up my mind. No one cared about me, so I had to protect myself. 'What are you looking for?' Ruby asked when she saw me searching around the garbage pails on our way. I didn't answer her. I really wanted her to go on. But Ruby, sensing something strange in my manner, walked alongside of me, stopping every time I stopped.

Finally I found what I wanted. Lying in an alley between two buildings was a pile of old plumbing. On top of the pile was a lead pipe just the correct size to squeeze into my book bag.

'What are you doing with that pipe?' Ruby asked. I kept on stuffing it into my bag without answering. 'I ask you, Phyllisia, what do you think you are going to do with that pipe?' I still did not answer. 'Phyllisia, I hope you didn't take your father's joke yesterday for truth?

39

He did not mean what he said, you know?' Hugging my precious bag to my chest I walked on. 'Phyllisia, those kids will tear you to pieces if they see you with that thing. I'm going right back home and tell . . .'

'Hey, Ruby, wait up for me.' It was one of the girls that went to Ruby's school. Ruby's friends were all glamorous. They all wore their hair long, curling on their backs. They all had well-shaped legs pushed tightly into sheer stockings. This girl looked like all the rest. When she walked up, Ruby left me without a second thought.

Jealousy pricked me. In a part of my mind I *had* wanted Ruby to run back home to tell Mother what I was about to do. Mother would have rushed after me, trying to stop me and might even have made me go back home. But just like that, Ruby forgot all about me and my pipe. She and her friend, full of secrets, walked on together. There was nothing left to do but go on with my plan.

Calvin had said to grab *one*. There was no doubt in my mind that the one had to be Big-Tits. If I grabbed someone else and left *her* free, she could attack me from behind. When I saw her I had to walk right up to her and give it to her good. But when would that be? Before or after school? It did not matter. I had to be prepared no matter when. Unzipping my bag so that my pipe would be easily reached, I marched grimly towards school.

'Hey, how ya doin'?' I looked up quickly, then as quickly looked away. It was that girl Edith. 'They sure did you in, huh?' Edith, still popping away at her bubble gum, gazed into my swollen face. 'Oh wow – I heard about it yesterday, but it was long after it happened or I

40

would have *been* back.' She fell in step beside me. 'What was it all about?' She waited a moment and when I did not answer snapped, 'It ain't no use you acting all hinky with me. I ain't done nothing to ya. I'm your friend.'

Hugging my book bag closer to my chest, I searched around for something to say in answer to that bold assertion. But Edith kept on, 'I hear it was that old big-tittied Beulah who started it. What you do to her?'

'Nothing,' I answered because it was simpler than ignoring her. Then I heard myself adding, 'She just doesn't like me. None of the children in that class like me.'

'I like you.'

'They don't like the way I speak.'

'What? I think you talk pretty.'

'You do?'

'Yeah, real pretty.'

This unexpected compliment gave me a rush of pleasure. I felt suddenly warm and friendly towards Edith. But then I looked down and saw her run-over shoes, saw the gaping holes in her stockings, and in annoyance I thought *if* someone *had* to like me, why it couldn't be Marian, or someone like Ruby's silk-stockinged friend.

'My mother is coming to school today,' I said as payment for her compliment.

'What good that's gonna do?' Edith popped her gum. 'Beulah'll just say that you are a mamma's girl and pick on you even worse.'

I hugged my book bag closer, wondering if I dared tell her about my pipe, while Edith kept on talking. 'But don't you worry about a thing,' she said. 'I'll fix them.'

'You!' Edith was certainly no match for Beulah.

Edith was shorter than I. She was wiry instead of muscular. Her square face did have an obstinate chin, but it was impish rather than tough. 'What can you do?'

'Never you mind. I'll fix them. They ain't got no right messing with no friend of mine.'

The classroom was in turmoil. All of the students were talking about the same thing at the same time: the fight. Miss Lass kept rapping on the desk with her ruler for order. But the bell had not yet rung and the boys and girls were taking full advantage of their free time for a bout-by-bout description of the fight. Having left Edith outside talking to a friend, I walked alone into the room and was greeted by a chorus of loud boos and shouts. 'Look at that eye,' someone shouted. 'She got a real tinger-linger-ringer-ooooh.' I walked stiff-backed to my seat.

Miss Lass had obviously been told about the fight for she gave my face a rapid, underhanded examination, then pretended she had not seen me.

When Beulah came in, a cheer went up. She came right to me. 'You think that you're so hot with that monkey fighting, huh? Well, let me tell you one thing. You ain't gonna have a chance to hit nobody with that head of yours unless you throw it straight when I hand it back to you.'

'That's right, Beulah,' a boy shouted from the back of the room. 'You tell it to her.'

Beulah swaggered to her seat, flopped down, banging her desk. The class went wild with applause. All my confidence in the pipe ebbed. It was the hostility of the class more than Beulah's threat which made me go limp with terror.

'Listen you,' the teacher shouted in exasperation, 'whatever you do in the streets, you leave out there, do you hear? When you come into this classroom, I want silence!' The bell rang and the children began to settle down into an uneven silence. The teacher repeated, 'What you do out in the street is your business. In this classroom you give *me* your undivided attention.'

I stared at my folded hands on the desk so that I would not have to see her face. This was the person that Mother was coming to see! What good would it do if this was the way American teachers cared for their students? Let them trample me, kill me, as long as it was in the streets and not in the classroom.

Beulah, to prove her absolute power in the classroom, ignored the teacher. She stood up, banging her desk loudly, then walked to the back of the room where she stood leaning over a boy's desk talking to him. The class snickered. Miss Lass threw her ruler angrily on the desk. But she pretended that she had not seen Beulah. At this moment Edith walked in, and Miss Lass's fury turned on her.

'Oh, Miss Jackson,' she sneered. 'So you have decided to honour us with an early appearance this morning. Tell me what or whom can we thank for this?'

Strolling to her desk, Edith threw her books on it. She then walked to the front of the room where she faced the class, her hands on her hips, her back to the teacher. 'Yeah,' she said, 'I came early this morning because I got a bone to pick with some people and I want to pick it clean.

'I hear tell that some of you been messing with a good friend of mine. Well, let me tell you one thing. If anybody in this room feel like messing with a monkey chaser, I got your monkey and I got your chaser. So come on and try me.' She chewed hard on her gum, hands still on her hips, one foot patting the floor.

I waited for Beulah to walk up to her. But Beulah didn't. Furtively I glanced back, saw her standing frozen over the boy's desk. Edith looked all around the room before letting her gaze rest on Beulah. 'If you don't take me on, you're a shit-eater!' Beulah still did not move. Edith blew a big bubble, pulled the gum into her mouth with her tongue, then said: 'O.K., looks as though ain't no bad mothers' daughters in here. But if you can't get bad in here, you ain't bad!

'And one more thing. That girl Phyllisia is my friend. My best friend. If anybody hits on her, they hitting on me. And that goes for if I'm here or if I ain't. Or if I'm early or if I'm late.' This last she threw over her shoulder to include Miss Lass, then she made her way to her seat.

The stunned silence in the room held. I felt the veins at my temples and my heart beating as one. I kept my eyes on my hands on the desk waiting for something to happen, an explosion, a battle cry, anything but the silence. Moments ticked by, and slowly, very slowly the tension in the room loosened. Whispers stirred the air like a warm breeze.

The girl behind me bent across the aisle to Edith. 'You sure did tell *her* off.' Edith blew a big bubble that burst leaving gum on her nose. She busied herself trying to rub it off. The girl touched my shoulder. 'Hey, Phyllisia. You know what happened yesterday wasn't my fault. I wish you'd tell Edith that it wasn't my fault. You know I never bothered you.'

It was too hard to believe. I didn't know whether to be happy or sad. I glanced back to where Beulah hung over the boy's desk. Incredible! She no longer looked belligerent. She looked defeated, unsure of herself. Walking the length of the room back to her seat must have been hard for her. Children averted their eyes as she passed. They dug their elbows into their neighbours' sides. They made stupid little gestures in their seats as though to avoid touching her. Many of the children looked over to me and smiled. I actually felt their hostility towards me fizzle.

Edith had not looked at me. Yet I realized I had to say something to show my gratitude. I forced myself to turn, meaning to talk, but found myself instead looking over her clothes: her badly wrinkled skirt, her unpressed blouse tied in front like a halter so that every time she moved, a band of brown skin showed between blouse and skirt. My feeling of gratefulness changed to one of annoyance. Did this mean then that I actually had to accept this girl's friendship? Why, she might even want to make it a habit of walking the streets with me!

I had no chance to look away. She turned and caught my eyes, gave me her open-faced grin and a mischievous wink. I knew then that I could never again turn from her in distaste, that I had to pretend at least that I accepted her friendship. My annoyance changed to anger. Who had asked her to butt into my affairs anyway! I could take care of myself. I did, after all, have my pipe.

6

I had no intention of becoming friends with Edith.

I did talk to her – keeping her at a distance and sometimes, when she came to school, she insisted on walking me a block or so on my way home. But I had more important things to think about than Edith.

For a long time I had been moving towards a feeling that everything was not right at our house. A word dropped here, a hint there, and a picture was slowly forming in my mind. Then one night while I was sleeping deeply, the picture was suddenly complete. I awoke and stared, through the darkness, at the ceiling. Something was wrong with Mother. Something was very, very wrong.

On our way to school the next morning, I broke a long, thoughtful silence to ask Ruby, 'How do you think Mother is?'

'How you mean how I think?' Ruby snapped with unreasonable fury.

'I mean, don't you think she is – don't you think that she acts strange?'

'What damn foolishness you want to push in my head?' she cried. I looked covertly around, not wanting to broadcast my suspicions.

'It's not foolishness,' I whispered. 'I think Mother is sick.'

'You're the sick one,' Ruby said, disregarding my attempt at secrecy. 'You are sick in the head and a jack-ass besides.'

We parted, Ruby stomping off towards the subway and I towards school, furious that I hadn't clouted her on the head for talking to me that way.

In the classroom, the heat and the restlessness of the children writhing in their seats or finding excuses to walk around the room attempting to look out of the windows did nothing to quiet my anger. Radio, television and newspapers had been talking about the 'long, hot summer' and the big riots that the heat would precipitate. Now the children were actually waiting for the hot sidewalks to explode.

Even Miss Lass was affected. She too kept glancing nervously out of the window, then walking back to her desk, her red face flushed from the heat, veins on her neck protruding as though she were shouting inside herself – while her crafty eyes darted around the room in search of a victim.

I kept thinking of Mother as she looked during breakfast. I was sure that I was right – particularly when remembering how she acted before leaving The Island. I had been nine. She used to tease me so much. I remember her putting her mouth at the base of my neck and blowing hard so that the wind of her breath tickled me, making me laugh and wiggle. And how she used to race up the hill at the back of our house so full of life and high spirits. She always won.

This quiet, reserved grand lady, always thinking inside herself, was really new to me. Remembering that, another part of my mind suddenly saw Ruby the night before, fixing a pillow for Mother to lean back on. Ruby was brushing back Mother's hair and looking down at her with concern – a little too much – registered in her sorrowful, brown eyes. That was before I had gone to bed . . .

'Well, Miss Smith – Smithinsky.' Miss Lass had caught a victim near the window. 'You seem to have forgotten the route to your seat today.'

It was Carole Smith. Carole was one of the quietest girls in the class. It had to be a very hot day to force *her* away from her seat. But Miss Lass wouldn't think of that. 'Perhaps it is because you greased your hair so well this morning that things keep slipping your mind,' she said.

Carole's stiffly starched white blouse gleamed against the sunlight shining through the window. The oil of her well-pressed, tightly curled hair glittered. 'If you would take more time in oiling what's inside of your head instead of what's on top, your sense of direction might not slip.'

The restless room grew tense. Someone in the back muttered: 'Who do she think she is?' Carole Smith's face shone from the sweat of her embarrassment. And the shame that she was experiencing, because of her oily hair, her sweating face, became my shame.

Turning from Carole, Miss Lass caught sight of me with that expression spread over my face – and abruptly it was my turn. 'Ah, Miss Cathy,' she sneered. 'Tell the class exactly what you were thinking as you so insipidly stared at Miss Smith's oily face.'

Leafing through all of the bittersweet, acidly polite, smart remarks that I had stored up for just such an occasion, I stared at her.

'Come, my brainy one,' she taunted. 'What has become of all your intelligence? Has it gone to the bottom of your feet? Or are you sitting on it?'

Shaking with anger, I fought against the habit of politeness. But the words trembled at the tip of my tongue, aching to be formed – and they might have been if Edith, coming in at that moment, had not saved me. For Miss Lass seeing her favourite target whirled around, greedily, to greet her.

'Can you tell me, Miss Jackson, why your mother even bothers to send you to school?'

Edith, popping her bubble gum, called over her shoulder. 'I ain't got no mother.'

'No,' Miss Lass shouted as though the heat had taken the better part of her reason. 'I wouldn't think that you did have a mother!' Then looking over the classroom she included us all in her assault. 'The way most of you come to school I wouldn't think that any of you had mothers. You come to school like pigs! Greasy, oily, filthy pigs! The filth in your streets shows what kind of people you are!'

We were all struck dumb. No one moved – no one could. After a painful, long silence, a boy at the back of the room finally muttered just loud enough for her ear, 'Your *mother* is a pig!' Someone from another part of the room hissed, 'She ain't nothing but a Jew!' Someone else put it into song, 'Miss Lass is a Jew-u.'

The teacher bristled. A snakelike movement of her hair uncoiled it from its bun. Her flushed face darkened to the colour of a beet, veins strained out of her neck like ropes and foam bubbled at the corners of her mouth. 'Let me tell *you* what people – decent people – call you,' she screeched.

The entire class responded. 'Miss Lass is a Jew-u.' Desks banging down in unison, voices loud, louder. 'Miss Lass is a Jew-u.'

Pity for the woman, standing before us like a wild, trapped animal, mixed with my anger. How could we do this to anyone? How could she do this to us? Before I knew what I was doing, I had grabbed my books and fled from the room.

It was confusing. Why should I care how hurt she was? She had insulted me. She had made me ashamed because I, like the rest of the class, happened to be born with the kind of hair that needed oil for its care. Foolish woman, lumping all of us together, calling us pigs. Why indeed should I care what they called her?

The chanting voices and the desks banging in rhythm followed me down the stairs, rang in my ears even after I left the building and was racing up the street.

'Phyl, hey Phyl, wait up.' Edith came after me. 'Boy, you sure took *off*. I didn't know you could run like that.' We fell in step. After a few seconds she said, 'I sure am glad they told that old heifer off, ain't you?'

'I thought it was awful.'

'What was so awful about it? She ask for it, ain't she? She been asking for it.'

'Yes, but . . .'

'But nothing. If she didn't want it, she oughtn't to have ask for it. People get what they ask for, you know? Least that's what I hear tell.'

I had been on my way home to Mother. Somewhere in my mind, earlier, I must have made up my mind to leave school, or how had it been so easy to just pick up and go? Perhaps it was Edith's presence that reminded me that home was the last place I should go. Calvin might still be there, or might just be leaving for the restaurant. If he saw me out of school, at this hour, he would backhand me first and ask questions later. With that in mind I turned and walked the other way. Edith changed directions too.

'Yeah,' she kept talking and popping gum. 'Old lady Lass sure did get hot. D'you see her face? I thought sure she would snap her wig. Someone ought to have done that long ago.'

'How can you tell that Miss Lass is a Jew?' I asked.

'Who cares what she is?' Edith asked, surprised.

'But the rest of the kids seem to know.'

'Look, it don't matter what she is. When you want to get even with whitey, just call them dirty cracker or Jew, and that gets 'em.'

I refused to show my stupidity by asking why. Edith seemed so casual and so wise with her pronouncement. But as we walked along, and I kept comparing my appearance with Edith's, my pity for Miss Lass changed back to anger. What nerve lumping us together! Pigs? Indeed her mother was one.

It was hot on the streets, but, worse, it was dangerous. I didn't know what corner Calvin might pop around. My nerves were jumpy and I imagined seeing him at every corner. The most sensible thing for me to do was to ditch Edith. Alone I could think up some kind of reason for my not being in school, which wouldn't be believed if I had company. But, for the first time since I had known her, I wanted her with me.

'Sure looks as though something'll be popping around

here soon.' While I had been on the lookout for Calvin, Edith had been studying the people grouped together on the streets. All the streets were crowded, mostly with older boys – talking and gesticulating wildly in the heat that seemed to bounce off the concrete buildings and simmer vapourlike among them, releasing the sweat that poured down from their brows and ran down their open-necked shirts.

'Popping?'

'Yeah. You know. Them long hot summers?'

We walked on in silence, then she asked, 'You ever been in a riot?'

'Uhuh,' I answered absently. I was thinking of The Island with its density of trees to lie under when the sun was hot. There were also little water holes where you could swim instead of going to the beaches. And if you were brave enough to slip out of school, there were always the coconut groves where one could play around until time to go home. 'Don't you have anywhere to go in New York?' I asked.

'Like where?'

'Like out of these streets.'

'We can always go to the movies.'

'We need money for that.'

'What about a subway ride? I got money enough for that.'

'I've never been on a subway.'

'Never on a subway?'

'No. My sister goes to school every day by subway. But I've never been on one. We just came here, you know?'

'But I thought everybody's been on a subway.'

52

'My father has a car. He takes us out in it. That is, *when* we go out.'

'Great, then I'll take you on your first subway ride. You'll like it. It's boss.'

We had come to the subway by this time, and I let Edith lead me down the stairs. She ducked under at the turnstile, dragging me with her. We straightened up under the disapproving stare of an elderly lady and Edith pulled me from under the severe gaze down to the other end of the platform. I was impressed by the way Edith had of not seeing grownups.

Being on the train was like being closed up in darkness, but as we roared uptown, the newness of the ride made everything exciting. Every time Edith said something I had to lean forward and yell at her to repeat. Finally we gave up talking and Edith opened her mouth and said 'awwwwww.' I opened my mouth and said 'awwwwwwwww,' and the train was not so noisy any more.

We rode a long time making noises and giggling, and suddenly I found that I was really having fun. I liked Edith. I really liked her.

Coming out into the light as the train track became elevated, we looked out at people walking below, people working in their little stores or standing talking in the hot sun, peeped into apartments where housewives worked, at people resting on their beds, at some sitting near windows reading in the fretwork of sunlight coming through the tracks. Small children waved as we passed and we waved back. We got off at the last stop. Bronx Park.

Edith took me to the Zoo. She bought me hot dogs

and we ate strolling around looking at animals. Edith knew everything about New York. She knew about Central Park and Mount Morris Park and the Museum of Natural History.

I was fascinated. I had never really seen Edith before. Now I noticed the little dimples that settled at the sides of her mouth when she spoke, her eyes black and shiny – big as saucers – with the black wiping out most of the white. She was really pretty. If only she would dress right. If I could save up some money I would buy her things – at least a pair of socks. The big holes at her heels were constantly on my mind. I imagined everyone saw them and kept looking at them when we passed.

On our way back Edith bought candy – Peter Paul Mounds. It was the best candy I had ever eaten, and because I loved it, Edith insisted on getting off at every stop with a candy stand to buy more. We ate Peter Paul Mounds all the way back to our stop.

When we left the subway, the streets were even hotter and louder as well as more crowded than when we left. Police cars cruised through the streets and mounted policemen guided their horses listlessly up and down. Edith looked around and said: 'Yeah, sure's going to be some happenings tonight.'

'Have *you* ever been in a riot?' I asked.

'Sure. Plenty times.'

'What happened?'

'Well, I'll tell you. It's like this. It all depends on if you are in the right place at the right time. And I usually am.'

We hooked arms and walked slowly up the broad main street, our heads close together. Gone was all fear of Calvin seeing me. I didn't even think of Calvin. It was just the most beautiful thing to have a really and truly best friend – a friend that you could enjoy. And I enjoyed Edith. I described Ruby to Edith and told her how glamorous Ruby was – but how she thought she was so much, and we talked ceaselessly about Miss Lass.

After we had walked two blocks up the main street we turned into the five-and-ten-cent store, and happy to be out of the heat and in the air-conditioned coolness, we joined other shoppers going from counter to counter.

We had spent all of Edith's money and so had no serious intention to buy. But although it was late – past the time I should have been home – I did not want to leave my new friend.

And so we examined items at the counters and talked, Edith walking slightly in front of me making little rapid gestures with her hands – gestures so charming I thought to imitate them. She stretched her hand languidly over the counter. I stretched mine over the counter. Carelessly, she picked up a pencil sharpener. The nearest thing to my hand was an eraser. I picked that up, waiting for her to throw down the sharpener in that casual manner which seemed hers alone. But she put her hand to her chest and when it came back her hand was empty!

My knees grew weak and my feet became immovable objects locked to the floor. Still I did not realize what I had seen, or thought that I had misinterpreted what I was actually looking at. A little further on she picked up a handful of pencils and in the same way made them disappear!

My friend Edith was a thief!

7

Still chatting, Edith had walked the length of the counter before realizing that I was not behind her. She turned, saw me staring at her and walked back. 'What's wrong with you, girl?' My mouth opened and closed, no word came. 'Come on.' She took my hand leading me and I stumbled after her, too numb to protest.

But I knew every eye in the place was on us, accusing us, and all I could do was follow. I was here with Edith and I was as guilty as she. My heavy lids forced my eyes to the floor. But I had to get out! What could I do? I forced myself to look up, look around, and then I saw, as though through a maze, Calvin coming towards us. My heart fluttered like a fan, a scream pushed up from my stomach and gurgled at my throat. I grabbed hold of the counter for support. The man feeling my gaze on him, looked at us, looked over us and turned at the next counter. I went limp with relief. It was not Calvin.

By this time, Edith, puzzled over my behaviour, put a practised little hand to my forehead and not liking the cold, clammy feel of my skin, said in a brisk voice: 'You feel as though you're sick, girl. Let's get the hell out of here.'

She pulled me towards the exit. I stumbled after her, expecting at any moment to feel a hand descend on my shoulder, to hear a gruff voice shout, 'Hey, you two,' to see someone dart out in front of us, threatening, calling to the policemen lining the streets outside, pointing at us, shouting, 'There they are. There go those thieves.' We reached the exit and walked out of the store. No one stopped us.

As I felt the hot, humid air on me, surrounding me like arms, my confidence came surging back and with it all of my former revulsion, my dislike for Edith. I yanked my hand from hers.

'Which way are you going?' I said coldly.

'That way.' She pointed towards Eighth Avenue.

'Well, I'm going this way.' I pointed towards Seventh Avenue although I lived midway between Eighth and Seventh Avenues and Edith knew it. It didn't matter, I would never talk to her again. Without another word I walked away.

She ran after me, grabbed my hand. 'Phyl, I don't think it would be too hip to go that way.'

'Don't touch me,' I cried pulling away. 'Don't you ever put your hand on me again, do you hear?' I wanted to say more. I wanted to say 'dirty' hand, to call her a nasty little thief. But I didn't. Perhaps I had liked her too much during the day. But my words had the same effect. Her large eyes registered instant pain. She opened her mouth to speak, but I turned proudly away and worked my way through the multitude of people now jamming the steaming sidewalk.

Then it happened. What the children, the teacher, even Edith had been waiting for. The sidewalk exploded. There was a hush – everyone stopped talking and breathing at the same time – then as though a rubber band had been cut, bodies shot out of everywhere at the same time.

One shout heaved to the heavens, and like a roaring wave, bodies slammed against me, pushing me backwards, forcing me off my feet, yet holding me upright by sheer numbers, the pressure of movement. Policemen on horseback rode into them, swinging clubs, policemen on foot waded in and broke up the wall of human flesh into smaller, more manageable knots. My support gone, I fell to the sidewalk. Feet stumbled over me, people tripped and fell, pulled themselves up and rushed to join whatever was going on over my head. Twice I tried to scramble to my feet, was knocked down and crouched, holding both hands over my head – my elbows meeting in front of my face – terrified, knowing that I would be trampled to death by the sightless mob.

'Get up. Get up.' I heard a voice in my ear, felt a hand tugging me up, upward. 'Hey, help! Help me, somebody! Get her up! Can't you see she'll get killed? Help me . . .'

Strong arms lifted me, helped me gain my footing. I opened my eyes. And there was Edith, hovering over me, her wiry little body a shield between me and the on-rushing tide. The strong hands disappeared as miraculously as they had appeared and I was once again firmly in Edith's grasp, being pulled here, tugged there, stopped, then yanked through little openings in the raging human surf.

I followed meekly, clinging to her strong little hands, knowing that my life depended on her. We somehow worked our way to the corner. 'Look,' Edith said. 'I live right up the avenue apiece. We gonna make it there and you can stay until this mess dies down and then I'll take you home.'

She took me over completely and I let her, grateful that some higher being had stopped me from saying all those nasty things I had wanted to say a little while before.

We manoeuvered up Eighth Avenue for a short distance before Edith stopped and pointed. 'See that stoop, Phyl? The third from here. That's where I live.'

A battle was raging on that stoop. Men, women and a force of police were tangled in one ferocious heap. 'When I say *now*,' Edith directed, 'pick up your feet and follow me.' Even with my confidence in Edith I couldn't see how it was possible. 'Don't worry,' she said, feeling me stiffen. 'The fighting will shift from there in a little while. It always shifts. Just be ready to move when I say.'

I looked around in despair, from this end of the street where traffic was snarled, cars were overturned, to the opposite end of the street where police on the sidewalk had cornered gangs of youths, lining them along the buildings. My gaze rested on one person and remained fixed on him because somehow he seemed familiar. It took a long time to realize that he looked familiar because he was. My father.

Calvin! At the sight of him standing on the stoop, the well-dressed observer at a bullfight, my terror took another form. No more was I the helpless victim of a horde – I became again an individual, Phyllisia, wanting to fade away. I crouched against a building. The fighters whom I had been trying to avoid now seemed less awesome, I tried to hide behind them – but he saw me.

The intensity of my stare must have drawn his attention. His eyes flicked in my direction, flicked away, then back again. I saw him give a start, push his neck out as though to clarify his vision. Then he left the safety of his stoop and began clearing a way, coming across the street towards me. A policeman on horseback bore down on him, swinging a club. Calvin's hand shot out. He seized the club, pulled. The policeman's horse reared . . .

'Now,' Edith was shouting. 'Now.' I needed no urging. I flew after her, to her stoop and into the house. I looked back once, but the crowd had closed Calvin from my view.

Edith and I ran up three flights of stairs, hearing footsteps drumming up behind us. I had no idea if it was Calvin chasing us or simply someone getting in out of the fight as we rushed into her apartment and then stood pushing hard against the door. The footsteps kept going up.

As we leaned there, out of breath, children came rushing at us from all corners of the room. 'Edy, Edy, you all right? You all right?' Everybody speaking at the same time. 'We seen the fighting and we think that you were sure enough in it and that something happen to you.' Edith walked jauntily.

'Sure I'm all right,' she bragged. 'What'd happen to me? Hell, I been in dozens of happenings. Ain't nothing never happen.' I thought I heard a quiver in her voice but she turned cheerfully to me.

'Hey, Phyl, these here my sisters. The big one there is Bessie. She ten. And this here is Suzy. She eight.' Edith touched each sister as she spoke. 'Minnie here is seven and that there is Ellen. She the baby. She four. I got a brother too. He out there somewhere. He older than me. Sixteen.'

Edith busied herself around the room we had entered.

It was a large room that served as a kitchen, bedroom and dining room. In one corner stood a black pot-bellied stove where Edith began making a fire. In another corner was a large sink filled with dirty dishes. A round table took up the centre of the room, surrounded by chairs, and along one wall was a bed which doubled as a couch.

I sat at the edge of the couch-bed, noticing how grown up Edith suddenly looked – not young any more – not old, just not young. It was as though the shadow of an old woman hovered over her but had not yet decided to stay. Her eyes, as she went about her chores, were no longer bright.

The house was just as shabby as Edith and her sisters. The pot-bellied stove reminded me of the poor people's outdoor stoves on The Island. Newspapers were stuffed into holes under the sink. How different this apartment was from ours. Our living room had a bright-red mohair couch. Our windows had ceiling-to-floor draperies, and Calvin never stopped bragging about how he had insisted, over Mother's objections, on covering the floors with wall-to-wall carpeting.

But then, why should I contrast Edith's house with mine? After all, Edith had saved my *life*. None of these things mattered.

At any rate, I did not feel my earlier horror when Edith began pulling pencils and other things from different parts of her clothing, including her panties. I did not feel the sin of it although I knew I should. Then the baby, Ellen, came and stood beside me. She put her elbows in my lap and looked up at me as though she thought I was the prettiest girl she had ever seen. My face and hands were dirty and bruised, my dress was filthy, yet she admired me! And just like that I knew that I didn't care a thing about Edith's sins.

Edith had taken a big pot from the icebox and put it on the stove, when the door opened and her brother came in, carrying a big ham. He was tall and slim with a pointed, intense face. 'That's my brother Randy,' she introduced him. 'Randy, this is Phyl.' Then eyeing the ham she added, 'That's what you call being in the right place at the right time.'

Randy did not speak. He nodded in my direction but kept a hostile stare, directed at an old rocking chair that was pulled up to the window, its back to the room.

Someone was in that chair! A man! I had not been aware of his presence, but now I noticed his feet, show- ing on the floor beneath the chair.

'Things are cooling down out there,' Randy said tak- ing his attention away from the chair. 'But I hear tell that a man's been killed and the police are beating heads and taking names. Say the hospital is full.'

A man killed? Up to that time I had taken it for granted that Calvin was running up and down like a madman looking for me. But at Randy's words, I saw again the police charging down on him. He hadn't escaped at all. He had been killed! I got to my feet. 'I better go home,' I said.

'You better wait a bit,' Edith cautioned, 'I'll take you home when it's time.'

'No, no, I must go now.' But just then we heard the backfiring of a car and Randy said:

'Listen to that. They shooting now.' I sat back down. I was afraid and ashamed of my cowardice. Why should I mind going out there when what had happened to Calvin was my fault? Everything was my fault. If I had not left school today, if I had not gone on that subway ride, if I had not gone to the five-and-ten – Calvin would be all right.

The least I could do now was to go to Mother. Stay with her when the news of his death arrived. What would I say to her? Strange how I hadn't thought of her for a long time, knowing she was sick too. Suppose something had happened since I left home this morning. Suppose she had become worried about me, about Calvin, and had gone out looking for us and had been caught in that terrible riot.

As I sat there, confronting my miseries, the old man got up. He was wispy with grey hair and cloudy eyes. Tired little steps took him behind the curtains to the other part of the apartment and when he returned he was wearing an old felt hat, pulled low over his brow. The little aching steps carried him to the stove, where he took a brown lunch bag, and then he walked out of the house. He had not said one word to anyone.

Bessie set the table and Edith insisted on fixing me a plate of black-eyed peas with neck bones, which I could not eat. How could I, with Calvin lying out there dead, and not knowing what had happened to Mother. But she heaped up the children's plates, even Ellen's – and I never saw a child so small eat so much.

But as I sat at the edge of the couch-bed, holding the plate, my mind was whirling with unanswered questions. Finally I could hold them no longer.

'Is – is he your father?'

'Yeah, that's him.' Edith's voice was as casual as ever.

'He on his way to work. He work mostly nights. Takes care of the kids when I'm at school.' Then after a pause she added. 'That is if they ain't sick. But they always sick with something or other.'

That explained her continual absence from school. A silence followed, broken by an occasional shot from outside and by spoons scraping at dishes inside.

'Where is your mother?' I asked.

'She dead.' Edith was just as casual but I was suddenly very frightened.

'Dead? How long?'

'Been about three years now. Ellen here was just one.'

Randy sent a hostile glance in my direction, resenting my questions, wanting me to shut up. I tried. But I heard my voice asking, 'Wa – was she sick long?'

'Yeah.' Edith stopped eating to explain to me. 'Long time. You know, she had TB. She ain't never stop ailing. Seems like since I first remember, I known she was going to die. And sure enough, one morning I went out to get the doctor and when I come back she was laying right down there – dead.'

'Right down there – down where?'

'Right there where you sitting. Right there on that selfsame bed.'

I know that I jumped up from that haunted bed, opened the door, ran down three flights of stairs, crossed all of those streets between Edith's house and mine. I know that I flew through streets without seeing anyone, hearing anyone – and my consciousness came back only as I was stumbling up the stairs to my apartment.

8

'I tell you, I grab him so. Man, he come flying.'

His voice! Loud and bragging it rushed at me as I opened the door. 'Yes, man, now I turn so . . .' I slipped into the apartment and tiptoed to the living room. Yes, there he was, bigger than life itself.

Mr Charles and Cousin Frank were there too. Along with Ruby and Mother they formed an awestruck audience.

'. . . and here another one coming. I move so – to one side and I reach to the other side. I had him.'

I edged into the room, and easing my way towards Mother, sitting on the couch, I wormed a seat between her and the arm. She smiled down at me, questioning with her eyes, yet never dropping her attention from the centre of the floor. At any rate she was all right – the same as I left her this morning.

'. . . his own horse kick him in the head. I tell you, you never see such a thing in your life.' Calvin did not look in my direction.

My fears, or reasons for fearing, kept dropping off one by one. Perhaps, after all, Calvin had not seen me out there in all that commotion. I had just imagined it as I had imagined seeing him in the five-and-ten. Slyly, I studied each face, so intent on Calvin's performance. No. No one indicated – not even by a flicker of an eye, that they had heard I did something wrong – or for that matter, that I had even overstayed my time. I was safe.

'. . . then two big, Irish-looking ones come charging. Oho, I say, that's the way you want it? That's the way you'll get it. I take their two little sticks, throw them away. Then I grab one by the collar, the other by the shoulder. I mash their heads together, so! You should hear the crack.'

Familiar objects settled into place around me: the drapes, pulled all the way back to let in air; the highly waxed coffee table with Mother's doodads bowing and shaking to the volume of Calvin's roaring voice; and Calvin, standing in centre-floor, smiling, awaiting his applause. I was home.

A thoughtful silence prevailed. A silence that respected Calvin's right to blow up incidents just a bit – but no one doubted him. The little patch on his head was living proof that he had participated in the fracas. What would they say if they heard about *me*. After all, I had a bigger part in the riot than Calvin! Suppose I stole the floor from him, told them that I was actually there when it *started*, how I had almost been killed, and how *my* girl friend had held off hundreds of people to save my life. Dared I? I stared down at my soiled dress, touched my skinned knuckles.

'Man, I tell you – I there minding me own business. People to the right of me breaking things. People to the left of me breaking things. People all around raising all kinds of bacchanal, and they pick me. Me!' He put both hands to his chest.

Cousin Frank laughed. 'I guess they couldn't tell the difference between the great men and the lesser ones in all of that excitement.'

'You can say that again,' Mr Charles agreed. 'Can you imagine dragging Calvin through the back door of Harlem people's troubles?'

'That's some comedown, huh, Calvin?' Cousin Frank teased. 'All the time you think you just making money off them, now to find you're one of them.'

Calvin smiled broadly. He was too pleased with himself to take offence.

'Eheh, well, here's the little Miss.' To my annoyance Cousin Frank turned the spotlight on me. 'We were just bringing out a search party to look for you.'

Calvin turned to look at me in amazement as though just aware of my presence. 'You could have knocked me down with a twig. I look up and who I see in the thick of things but this one.' He came to me and pushed his face down next to mine. 'But tell me one thing. How is it you come to be in one part of town when you school is way the next?'

The suddenness of the question, when I had been so sure that I was home free, sounded warning bells all through me. Still, there was no anger in his eyes, so I decided to match his casual tone. 'I walked out of school today,' I replied.

The silence descending over the room, the twitching of Calvin's eyebrows, showed me my mistake. But once started, there was nothing to do but push on.

'The teacher called us pigs and said our mothers were pigs,' I said desperately. 'I knew that you wouldn't want me to listen to talk like that – about Mother – so I walked out.'

My words had no visible effect, so I bypassed the time of day I had actually walked out and all other events in between to get to the hair-raising part of my story. I had to enlist everyone's sympathies. 'My friend walked out too. I was with her when the fighting broke out and I . . .'

'Your who?' Calvin interrupted.

'We were right in the middle . . .' I wanted desperately to tell of how I had fallen and how Edith had saved me.

'Your *who* did you say?'

'My – my . . .' It was not going to work. I knew it.

'But you mean to say that teachers talk to children like that in class?' Mr Charles' indignant question came to my rescue.

'Oh God, but I never hear such a thing,' Cousin Frank backed him up. 'But, Calvin, you permit this?'

'Who permit what?' Calvin asked.

'You. Are you not a parent?'

'Me?' Calvin grew defensive. 'How I know how teachers talk?'

'You don't make it your business to find out?' Mr Charles prodded. 'That's what's wrong with these New York schools. Parents allow teachers to get away with murder.'

'Me – me,' Calvin sputtered, annoyed over his diminishing popularity. 'Who come to me to tell me anything?'

I wanted so much to hasten his demise by shouting: No one can tell him anything. But my luck was running too well.

'Why do you think that you get these damn riots all the time, all the time so?' Cousin Frank kept pushing the argument. 'It's by people letting everything, everything go and go until one day it spill over.'

'But you know me – Charles – Frank,' Calvin pleaded 'I ever stand for nonsense? No! I tell you I will be at that school tomorrow to find out about this mess. Tomorrow! And if I don't get satisfaction from the principal, I will take it as high as the Mayor. You know me.' Calvin stalked out of the room.

I hugged myself. Was it possible that I was coming out of this nightmare of a day with only scraped knuckles to prove I had lived it? I looked around at all of their faces, still caught up in their indignation. Oh grownups, grownups, they were not so wise after all. I tried to keep serious but a laugh kept tugging at my face. So I leaned over, staring at the carpet to hide my satisfaction. But then I found myself staring down at a pair of men's shoes. I had not heard him re-enter the room.

Slowly raising my head I found myself looking at a finger pointing right between my eyes. I heard Calvin's voice saying: 'Your friend, huh? But you playing with me. You think I bring you to this man's country and set you down in good surroundings so you can make friends of these little ragamuffins. Just let me catch you with that girl again. And not only she, but any other one that look like she. See what happen to that fast little tail of yours. It will be so hot with fire that you will pray for the gates of hell!'

Part Two

9

'You mean your mother will let you wear silk stockings to school every day?' Edith exclaimed.

'Of course,' I answered. 'High school is not like junior high, you know? What would we look like going to high school in socks? And that's not all, heels too, high heels – well anyhow, medium. My sister, Ruby, wears them.'

We were in the park – Central Park. Edith was sitting with her back against a tree while I lay rolling on the cool grass looking up at the sky – blue sky made golden by the intense light of the midsummer sun. A short distance away, Edith's sisters, having made a ring around little Ellen, were singing in loud voices 'Little Sally Water'.

'Well,' Edith said doubtfully. 'I guess that I'll be looking after getting me some silk stockings. Anyway I got until September to think about that.'

'Sure,' I agreed, tempted to ask how she intended to get them. Instead I said deliberately, 'My mother says she's going to buy me a tan-coloured wool suit and a yellow blouse to go with it for the first day. It would be good if we both could dress alike.' We had chosen the same school and had taken the same subjects so that we would always be together.

Edith looked at me half wistfully, half wonderingly.

Then she turned away, letting her gaze travel to where her sisters were shrieking, 'Turn to the east. Turn to the west. Turn to the very one that you love the best.'

Blood rushed to my face and I followed her gaze to where little Ellen was squatting in the circle. I never really intended to hurt Edith, but there was this streak of wickedness that kept popping out of me. I didn't understand why. And Edith seemed to look right through me into my wickedness. But she ignored my statement to ask, 'How is your mother feeling?'

I let my thoughts stray to Mother and her distant, quiet attitude. She did not look any sicker. 'I – I don't know,' I answered. 'But I know one thing, I felt like staying home with her and I would have too, if you hadn't been here waiting.'

That was not exactly true. I missed many days of meeting Edith in the park when I could be alone with Mother. But today Ruby had come in with a friend and had begun to boss me around, so I left. However, my words succeeded in erasing from Edith's eyes the hurt I had caused. The dimples of her pleased smile dug in at the sides of her mouth. Her eyes shone. It was so easy to make Edith feel good.

'It must be boss to have a big sister take over when you're not at home.'

Shrugging I replied, 'Ruby is such a show-off. She loves to grandstand. If someone says. "Oh that Ruby, she is so helpful," she goes crazy.'

Snuggling down intimately next to me on the grass, Edith asked, 'Do your mother like your sister better than she do you?'

Staring up at the unblemished blue of the sky, listening to the children shout, 'Rise, Sally, rise. Sally, wipe your pretty eyes,' I turned that question over in my mind. 'No – no I don't think so.' I wanted to shout that Mother loved me better but I really didn't know. I thought that she did. Before Ruby had come in today, I had been reading to her and she had said to me, 'You are a strange mixture of so many things. A little like me. I used to love reading when I was young. But then you have this queer manner of secrecy and pride – interesting.' But Mother hadn't actually come out and said, 'I like you better.'

'Anyway, my father likes Ruby better. He's crazy about her. But he hates me. We hate each other.'

'Did you get home before he did yesterday?' It was a big game to us, my beating Calvin home. Of course no one ever knew the exact hour Calvin would check in on us. Sometimes he never even bothered to check up. But it added to the excitement of meeting Edith in the park – it was more fun.

'Yes, I did,' I answered. 'But you would know he had to have something to pick on me about. He raised one fuss because my hair had become unbraided.'

That was not exactly true. Calvin had simply brushed my hair back with one of his big hands and had said: 'Girl, why don't you tie this mop up if you have to be in the wind?' Then he had said, 'But where do you go to get so much wind?' And I had answered, 'In the park.' 'What park?' he had asked.

And I had lied, 'Mount Morris Park,' thinking of him taking two giant steps to cover little Mount Morris Park in search of me, while I was safely hidden in the middle of Central Park.

'Why is he so mean to you?' Edith asked.

'Because he says I'm ugly.'

'That's a lie!' It had become a game for Edith to defend me against the evil Calvin. 'You are nice-looking, Phyl. So nice-looking. I wish I had hair like yours.' She reached out and touched my soft, but too-thin, unmanageable hair. I was so pleased. I was always pleased around Edith and her sisters. They thought I was pretty, all except Ellen, the baby, and she thought I was 'beautiful.'

Smiling, looking up at the sky, I said impulsively, 'On The Island we have months of days like this.'

'Not in New York,' Edith answered. 'Every day here is different. Just watch, it's going to rain soon.'

'Oh no, it isn't. It can't,' I protested and Edith quoted, 'If the skies are a cloudless blue, it will rain in a day or two.' But she was always harping back to her favourite topic, the handsome and cruel Calvin. 'Tell me about your father's restaurant, Phyl. How big is it?'

Calvin had never taken us to his restaurant. I didn't even know where it was. I only knew it was big because it had to do with Calvin, and so I answered glibly, 'Oh it's big, gigantic!'

'And what about the waiters? Are they all dressed up and lead people to their tables?'

'Oh sure. Just like in the movies. They all wear these dark suits. And not only that,' I added, 'all the tables have white tablecloths and a bottle of champagne and caviar.'

'Wow, champagne and caviar! What does that look like?'

Unwilling to admit that I never saw caviar, did not even know what it was, I shrugged, 'Oh champagne, you know? It pops, and it flows all over when you open the bottle.'

'Can you take me there some time, Phyl?'

'No,' I answered truthfully. 'I couldn't. My father won't even let us go there. He says there are too many men. You know how he is with his precious Ruby – he thinks somebody will rape her or something.'

Edith sighed, 'It sure must be fun to be rich.'

I wondered how rich we really were. I knew Calvin's place was swanky, but I also knew he was having his problems. Just the other night I had heard Calvin and Mr Charles in one of their frequent arguments. Calvin had asked Mr Charles to lend him money, and Mr Charles had answered: 'Me, lend you money to open another place? But Calvin, you joking? True, I know you want to get as big as Rockefeller. Bigger yet. But let this place show a little profit before you branch out.' Calvin had shouted back, 'Charles, you think you're forward-thinking but you thinking backwards. Retreating senses is what you have! That's what's the trouble with you people. You never think big!

'I'm going to be one of the richest men in Harlem, Charles, with you or without you.'

No, I did not know how rich we really were. But I put it philosophically, 'Yes, but I guess being rich has its problems.'

'I wish my old man was like yours,' Edith said dreamily. 'But we just ain't never had no kind of money.'

'Like my father?' How dared she compare that little wisp of a man with Calvin! 'Nobody can be like Calvin!'

Then I added because of that strange hurt expression, 'Nobody can ever be so mean and hateful.'

Ellen clung to me as we parted at the entrance of the park – we always parted at the entrance of the park, Edith to go Eighth Avenue and I to go Seventh, so that Calvin would not by chance see us together.

'I want to go with Phyl. I want to go with Phyl.' Ellen was the sweetest little girl in the world. When she held me tight around my neck with her chubby baby arms, I knew that even if I had a little sister I could not like her half as much.

Edith, ignoring her for the time, went up to an old hunchbacked woman selling flowers near the curb. She came back and pushed a bunch of roses into my hand. 'Give these to your mother for me. Say it's from your best friend to the prettiest mother in the world.' Then grabbing the unsuspecting Ellen by the hand, she pulled her away before I had a chance to thank her or Ellen had a chance to protest.

Ruby's friend had gone and Ruby was preparing dinner in the kitchen when I came home. Mother was lying on the couch in the living room. She was not sleeping although her eyes were closed, nor did she open them when I stood over her. After a few minutes of standing there I called, 'Mother . . .' Her eyes opened and she stared without recognizing me. 'Why don't you go to bed?' Recognition came slowly, as though through a long period of time. 'Do – do you want me to make it down for you – I mean your bed?'

'My bed?' She spoke in such cold tones that I shivered. 'After all, Phyllisia, the living room is for the living – not the bed.'

Shifting my weight from one foot to the other, I stood there not knowing what to say. Then I remembered the flowers in my hand and held them out to her. 'For you,' I said. 'My friend – my best friend sent them.'

Her face softened. She sat up. 'How nice. How pretty.' She relaxed. 'You with your secrets. So you have a friend – a best friend?'

'She's my only friend.'

'But of course,' she smiled confidentially. 'One can't be secretive with many friends.' She seemed to be waiting for me to answer but I did not. 'In this way I think you are like me. I never had many friends.'

'You didn't?'

'No, I was a very lonely child. I never could think or act or be a part of any group. Be careful that you don't have the worst faults of your parents.' She laughed. But I felt a seriousness beneath, and I had it again, that earlier feeling that she was trying to say something beyond the ordinary exchange we usually had, that she was trying to forge a bond between us that had been missing since I had arrived in New York. Sitting beside her I searched for words to open this new confidence. But I had been kept at my distance too long. 'It was hard,' she continued. 'Life seems so much better if one is surrounded by friends.' She looked away towards the window. 'Perhaps it is, I don't know.'

I sat there, hardly breathing, grateful for the intimacy. I knew she was never that close to Ruby. 'But, Phyllisia, I cherish those lonely years. I did not have many friends, but those I found were the gems of my youth.'

This was the opening I needed to talk about Edith. How I wanted to tell her of how Edith had taken up for me in school and how Edith had saved my life the time of the riot. I wanted her to see Edith the way I did – pretty but poor, cooking and caring for a big family – something like Cinderella.

But all the while I was bursting to tell her these things, another part of my mind was stubbornly remembering the night of the riot – remembering how Calvin had threatened me about Edith and no one, not even she, had protested.

Now she was saying, 'But how is it? You have a friend and you don't bring her here to meet me? You must bring her. I want very much to meet her.'

And still I could not bring myself to talk about Edith. What if I did bring her and she did not like Edith's looks? Would she tell Calvin? And would they try to stop me from seeing my only friend? Did Mother ever keep secrets from Calvin?

I stared down at my hands because I could not look at her. 'She – she's so busy, Mother. She has so much to do. We only meet each other – sometimes – in the park.'

'One day, instead of meeting her in the park, invite her here.' She smelled the roses. 'Anyone who would buy such nice flowers for a mother they don't even know must be able to spare five minutes in meeting her.'

She's drawing me into a trap! She and Calvin planned this talk so they could find out what I was doing! Whom I was meeting! I got up and walked to the window. Mother's voice followed, 'You must promise that you will bring her to meet me.' My suspicions grew, at her insistence. 'Promise?' I nodded but crossed my index finger over the third to invalidate the promise.

Hot blood rushed to burn my face, my body, to

tingle the soles of my feet. I was making it all up. Mother would never try to trap me. She would never conspire with Calvin against me. I was making it up because I did not want her to see my friend. And I did not want her to see her because I was ashamed of Edith. I loved her but I was ashamed of her!

As the enormity of my betrayal of Edith hit me, it stunned me. I had to make it up to her. But how? How could I ever make up to her for all that she had done for me? I thought of our talk in the park. Stockings. Silk stockings. Tomorrow when I got my allowance I would go out and buy Edith a pair of silk stockings. It did not matter that school did not start until September. I had to buy them tomorrow and show her that I really and truly loved her. Tomorrow I would make it up to her for being ashamed of her.

10

But the next day it rained.

Clouds had come together from nowhere, during the night, and when I awoke in the morning, sheets of rain were pouring down in front of my window. I was imprisoned, and Mother was firm. I could not go out. I appealed to Ruby for support, but she, in her bossiest manner, joined in the refusal: 'What! Go out in that downpour? Do you want to catch pneumonia so that I have to stay in and take care of you for the rest of the summer? You must be mad!'

I spent the entire day sulking, staring out of the window, waiting for the rain to stop. Heaven itself was intent on punishing me for my attitude towards my friend. It did not stop. Nor did it stop the next day or the next.

But if the rain kept me in, it also kept Ruby's girl friends out. And Ruby could not bear loneliness. At first she tried to force her attention on Mother. But Mother tired easily, went into the back room, her sewing room, to close her out. Naturally Ruby turned to the only other person in the house, me. 'Phyllisia,' she ordered, as though she actually thought she could rule me, 'I want you to read to me.'

Distressed as I was over my confinement and angry with her for having sided against me, I had been waiting for her to approach me. I narrowed my eyes at her.

'You must have jumped out of your mind. I would quicker read to maggots making babies in filth.' I had thought of a much dirtier thing to say, but I knew it would only give her an excuse to rush back to Mother to tell.

Ruby was quiet for almost an hour. But as I gazed out of the window I could feel her restlessness mounting. It always surprised me how well I knew her. Without looking at her I could read her mind. I knew exactly when she would begin to plead.

'Oh come on, Phyllisia. Don't be that way.'

Determinedly, my stare fixed on the water filling up the gutter, sweeping debris like wrecks in a stormy sea into the sewer. She would be crawling on hands and knees begging pretty soon – and it was not that she really wanted me to read to her. She just liked to hear someone talking, something filling her head, all of the time.

It came to me then that maybe I could force Ruby to do whatever I wanted – like maybe giving me her allowance, and I could buy two pairs of stockings for Edith instead of one.

'Phyllisia, my God. You would think that I wanted you to put the world upside down. All I want you to do is read.'

'O.K. I'll read. But you must give me your allowance for this week.'

'What? Will you give me one good reason why you think that I really jumped out of my mind?'

'You want me to read, don't you?'

'Yes, that's a good reason. To want *you* to do anything is to be half out of my mind. To *expect* you to is to be jumping mad.'

I shrugged, going into our bedroom and curled up on the bed with a book. Ruby came to the door to see what I was doing, stood there for a few minutes, then went back to the living room. She was quiet. Then I heard her walk down the hall to Mother in the back room. It was only a question of minutes now before she would re-appear at the door.

'I want you to read to me,' she said. 'But not two whole dollars worth.'

'How much?'

'Fifty cents.'

I shook my head. 'I need at least one dollar.'

'Fifty cents this week and fifty cents next.' I shook my head, no. I could see myself getting money when Ruby's friends were around again! 'Why do you need so much money?'

'I'm in trouble.'

'What kind of trouble?'

'I can't tell you. But will you let me have it?'

'No.'

'But you don't need money, Ruby. You and your friends hardly go out. All you do is go to each other's houses to gossip.'

'We go to the movies.'

'Not every week.'

'If we want to we do.'

I shrugged, bent my head over the book. 'Anyway,' I said. 'You know how I hate to read out loud.'

'Fifty cents. Take it or leave it.' I thought I heard a note of finality in her voice so I decided to take it. After all, fifty cents was better than nothing. But no sooner had I started reading than Ruby interrupted me.

'Phyllisia, you know, there is a boy in my school. His name is Joseph. He thinks that I'm the prettiest. Sometimes he waits for me on the stairs and . . .'

I closed the book. Not even for Edith could I put up with that for fifty cents. 'One dollar or nothing,' I said and closed the book.

Resentfully, she gazed at me. 'They call that blackmail, you know.' I shrugged. We exchanged hard stares. 'O.K.,' she relented.

The fifth day opened with a rage of sunlight. I jumped out of bed, did my chores around the house with special care – so Ruby would not take out her spite on me by holding me up – gulped down my breakfast and rushed out of the house. But the stores had not yet opened.

I could not wait. Rushing to Edith's house, I rapped loudly on the door thinking to awaken her. We could go together to buy the stockings.

But everyone was already awake in Edith's house. They were awake and sitting around the kitchen table, still dressed in their nightclothes. Everyone appeared so solemn. No one rushed to greet me as was customary – not even little Ellen.

Guilt was my first reaction. Had they somehow found out about my conversation with Mother? But that was silly. How could they? Perhaps they were angry because I had not been around for days – and that after Edith had been nice enough to buy flowers for my mother. 'My mother wouldn't let me come out in the rain,' I apologized.

'We figgered that,' Edith said. Then something else was wrong.

'It's my old man,' Edith answered my unspoken question. 'He ain't here.' I glanced to the window. Randy stood there looking out. The rocking chair, as always, stood with its back towards the room, but the old man definitely was not in it. And because he was not, the room, to me, seemed less oppressive. 'He ain't been here for two days.'

Aren't they glad to be rid of him? I thought. But obviously not. They all looked sad. Even Randy. In my quick glance at him I could see he was not as hostile as usual. He seemed confused, puzzled. 'Pa ain't never done nothing like this before,' Edith explained. 'He ain't never stayed out one day. The first day, it was raining so hard, we just figgered he stayed where he work. But now, I don't know. I think something done happen to him.'

My surprise of the silk stockings hardly seemed worth mentioning now. It was still important to me, but I feared that at this moment it might seem frivolous to Edith. 'We been sort of waiting,' Edith continued. 'Thinking that maybe the folks where he work will come to let us know if something done happen on his job.'

'Where does he work?' I asked.

'Dunno. He been working the same place as long as I know. On some railroad or the other. Last night I went down to the subway station and asked the man how I could get to the railroad. He ask me which one. I ain't even known that there was more than one railroad.'

I stared at Edith wondering what was so different about her and then realized that she wasn't chewing her bubble gum.

'Are you going to the police?' I asked.

'You joking?' She was shocked at my suggestion.

'And having them all over this place poking around and getting nasty with us? No, girl.'

'But we got to go to the police,' Randy cried from the window. 'Because they get nasty sometimes don't mean they get nasty all the time. What else we gonna do?'

'You mean ain't nothing else *you want* to do.' Edith spoke scornfully. 'But not you or nobody else is getting no police to poke their noses in this here apartment.' Randy turned back to look out of the window. After a while he spoke again, 'But supposin' he never come back?'

'Yeah,' Edith snapped. 'Just supposin'.'

'What about the kids, Edy?' he asked.

'Yeah, what about them?' she flared back at him.

'They too young to be out here with just you and me to look after them.'

'You mean you scared that you might have to go to work or something?'

'It ain't nothing like that.' He whirled to face her. 'I ain't no cop-out.' They stared at each other angrily; then, 'But supposin' he sick somewhere or something done . . .'

Edith's small face hardened. She leaned across the table. 'If he's sick and in some hospital, he'll be back when he get well. If he ain't . . .' she paused, '. . . ain't nothing nobody can do about it, and bringing the cops to *this* house sure ain't gonna help.'

Did they really want that little old man back? I asked myself. Why should they when all he ever did was look out the window? And if they didn't, what was the use of getting the cops? I supposed that was Edith's thinking too, but I couldn't tell just by looking at her. She looked so domineering, her face so unreadable.

'And not only that,' she said flatly. 'We ain't gonna say nothing to nobody about it.' Then remembering that, possibly, I didn't come under her authority, she stretched her hand across the table to cover mine. 'You dig?'

I shook my head. 'Somebody should know, Edith. What if I told my mother.'

'Then she would rush to tell your father. And you know how mean and hateful he is.'

'I think that we should tell some grownup about it.'

'Like who?' I thought of Miss Lass – maybe we could find her. But then Miss Lass hated us so much. 'Phyllisia, grownups are funny people. They go around pretending to help just to mind your business. Tell one and before you know they will have the whole police force down on you. And you know what will happen then, don't you?'

'What?'

'The people will put us all in some kind of home.'

'What people?'

'The city folks, that's who. I know them, girl. It happened to some kids that lived in the next house. They took them away and nobody ever heard of them again.'

'But that was because both their folks was *dead*.' Randy had said that one word that no one wanted to hear. Silence rocked the room. Every eye in the place looked at Edith. She alone could unsay them. Edith moved her jaw as though searching for the wad of gum she used for assurance. Bessie broke the silence.

'Anyway, we ought to keep it secret until Pa does get back.'

An avenue of hope had opened and Edith turned her

black eyes to me, overwhelming me with their directness. 'I know about them places, Phyl,' she pleaded. 'They treat you so mean in there. Especially when you're black. They beat you and make you wash your hair with lye soap and they won't let you put no grease on it to comb it.'

I remained unconvinced. And Edith seeing it in my face, was determined to convince me. 'And besides, I told my mother I would always take care of these kids. Phyl, how would *you* feel if you made a promise to your mother and somebody – your *best friend* – made you break it?'

It was the *only* argument that could shake me. I *knew* that if I ever promised my mother something, the person who made me break it would be my worst enemy. Then I looked at little Ellen, sitting in the too-big chair, her chin raised and resting on the table, absorbing all of the discussion as though she understood the seriousness of all being said, her Edith-looking eyes frightened. Oh Ellen, Ellen, pretty little Ellen. How could I even think of doing anything to cause you to be put away – perhaps never see you again?

Edith saw the change in my expression. 'O.K., now we all have to raise our right hands and promise God and a stack of Bibles that we won't tell.' We all raised our right hands. 'Promise?'

'We promise,' her sisters said.

'Promise, Phyl?'

'I promise.'

Only Randy stared out of the window and did not promise. Edith did not insist. She knew she had him under control.

11

Edith dropped out of school that year.

I missed her but there was so much to take up my time that it was not easy to think of depressing things. It was my first autumn in New York. With the greens turned brown and browns to vivid reds sharp against the clear blue of the sky; with the air clear, sharp, tingling and infectious; going into a new school with new clothes – dark greens and tans and browns, matching the turn-about trees – squeaky new shoes; meeting new people; having a new teacher, everything was just too exciting.

Adding to my excitement, I found myself in the same class with Marian. Marian Robbins. Marian was much shorter, so she sat in the front of the room while I sat in the back. But we looked at each other over the heads of the other students and I knew we were going to be friends. I was not quite as pleased, however, as I might have been the term before – but then I already had a best friend.

At the end of the day, it was Marian who waited for me. We took the subway together and it was Marian, while we were walking down our street, who repeated for the tenth time, 'I was so glad to look up and see you sitting in my class. I've really been wanting to meet you for the longest.'

Remembering how hard I had tried to make friends

with her and how badly she had snubbed me, I merely said, 'I would have been lost on the subway if you were not with me.'

She must have remembered too for she hurriedly explained, 'I wanted to meet you last term but my girl friend was so funny. She said you talked too bad. I don't think you talk *that* bad. Anyway I'll get used to it.'

I flushed, wanting to tell her that she did not really have to. Instead I inquired, 'Where is your girl friend now?'

'Oh, she moved away. Her folks bought a house in the suburbs.'

'Oho,' I muttered, noncommittal. Marian rushed on to say:

'I was sure I would meet you last summer but you didn't hang around the block much.'

'No, I usually went to the park when I went out.' I thought about Edith whom I hadn't seen in two weeks. I had been so busy shopping and preparing for school.

After Edith's father disappeared, I had been second in command at Edith's house for a while. Dashing there to help prepare breakfast in the mornings and to prepare the kids to go out. It had been fun. Between Edith and me, we had pretended that nothing had changed. But as summer slipped by racing into fall, the change began to show.

First, Randy had found a job in the garment district. But Randy could not take orders. He ended up fighting with his boss and lost the job. Then Edith had to find a job. She began to work in people's houses. It was only to be for a time – until the old man came back. But he never did.

'I wasn't around all summer either,' Marian was saying. 'My father sent me to camp. My father is a lawyer, you know?'

How was I supposed to know when I had never spoken to her before? Still, I answered pleasantly, 'That's nice.'

'He doesn't like me to stay around the city in the summer, so he sends me to camp, and sometimes he sends me down South to stay with my grandmother.'

This I thought was very nice, so I answered, 'That's nice.'

'My mother doesn't like me to go away though. She misses me. I'm the only child, you know?'

'Oh?' I wondered if it was nice to be an only child. Ruby and I had always wanted a brother.

'It's a real drag being an only,' Marian said unconvincingly. 'I would rather have a house full of brothers and sisters. Say, you have a real gone sister.'

Of course Marian would think that. She and Ruby were the same type. 'Do you really think so?'

'Oh yes. All of the girls around here dig her the most. She's really on to something. I wear my hair like hers. Haven't you noticed?' I hadn't. Marian's hair was long and thick but not half as long or as thick as Ruby's. Nothing she did with hers would quite have the same effect. Not noticing my critical silence she babbled on like a brook. 'Yes girl, your sister is gone. Your mother too. My mother says that your mother is one of the best-looking women she has ever seen.'

'I'll tell her you said so.' I smiled, and wanting to return the compliment looked admiringly into Marian's eyes. But her eyes lacked expression. They did not have the levels of interest that had always forced me to probe into Edith's eyes, no intense fires to feed on. Her eyes were not even nearly as expressive as Ruby's. Hers were toneless, blinking with birdlike curiosity – an interest that remained on the surface.

Yet, Marian's clothes were lovely. Everything about her, the pores of her brown skin, her carefully arranged hair, shouted good care. No one would ever dare question Marian as a choice for a friend.

'My mother says that your father owns a restaurant. It will be great if we can go there to eat sometime.'

'Yes, it will be fun,' I agreed. We had come to my stoop. 'I'll talk to my father about it.' I watched her walking away, towards her house, not feeling particularly happy, and I wondered why. Perhaps it was because she liked everything about me but me, I reflected.

Ruby was already at home. 'Hey Ruby, guess what,' I shouted as I entered the living room.

'What?' Ruby snapped back. She was sitting, sulking, on the couch.

'You're setting style nowadays. My friend, Marian, you know that cute girl that lives up the block, across the street? Well, she's fixing her hair to copy yours.'

'So what?'

That kept me quiet. Forced me to study her. When Ruby did not bite and chew and grin over a compliment, something was really wrong. Her sad, soulful eyes – no, she was not really like Marian – showed hurt right down to her toes. 'Mother?' I asked. 'Where is she?'

'In the back room.'

'What is she doing? Sewing?'

'No, just staring out into the back yard.'

'Which way is she today?'

'Bright.' Ruby's lips were pulled down at the corners. I pulled mine down to match hers and slumped down beside her. When Mother was in what we called her 'bright' mood, the best thing was to leave her completely alone – a thing that Ruby could never do. Ruby had to keep pushing herself on Mother, insisting on doing this, that or the other. She never stopped until Mother gave her a good tongue-lashing.

'What happened?'

'She was looking tired, so I told her to go to bed. Then she called me selfish and self-centred and said I was trying to force her into her bier.'

'Oh dear.' I leaned back and simply let the oppressive atmosphere of the house engulf me. There was no use fighting against it.

I had come to believe that a person's thoughts and attitudes were so strong that they really imprisoned people. I had long made up my mind that I would devote my life to proving that if powerful enough lenses were developed, thoughts could be seen or heard, just like sights and sounds are picked up by radio or TV.

'She's just trying to be mean,' Ruby's unhappiness broke through my reflections. I put my arm about her shoulders. Ruby was really tender and easily hurt. Whenever anyone made her unhappy I forgot all of her faults.

'Don't trouble your head about her. One day she'll be sorry.'

My sympathy brought tears. 'She's so ungrateful. I do everything I can to please her and all she can do is scold.'

'That's all right. One day she'll need you and you won't be around.'

We were still taking comfort in that vague threat when Calvin came in. 'Where's your mother?' he asked, looking around the room as though she might be hiding in the air.

'In the back.' Ruby's sullen response made Calvin pause. He too hated Mother's 'bright' mood. But Mother had already heard him and she came down the hall to greet him.

'Ah Calvin,' she cried gaily. 'How you do keep me waiting. When you have news for me it seems to take you forever.'

'Ramona, you know I busy. What is it?' He had been showing signs of fatigue – darkened eyes and pushed-in hollows at his cheeks.

'Yes,' Mother kept up brightly. 'I take notice that you don't come around the house with your loud talk. I remember one time I used to look at you and wonder if you were in the restaurant business or in the talking business.'

Calvin chewed down on his lower lip reflectively, then decided to match her cheerfulness. 'Well, you see,' he joked, 'to succeed, a man must sometimes shut up his mouth and pull up his sleeves.'

'Nonsense, Calvin.' She would not let him better her. 'That is for other men, not you. You should go on and talk. Make plen-ty noise. The noise you make in this apartment makes you a man. When your noise is heard from one end of Harlem to the other, you will be a great man.'

'And I guess you think that when my noise is heard from one end of the country to the other, I will be a dead man.'

It was eerie, their efforts to outdo each other. Great

humour without laughter. Yet their talk was animated. Their faces stretched out rubberlike, in smiles. She even laughed. 'But never be silent, Calvin. Never be silent. When you become silent, you will be a failure.'

But he fell silent now – suddenly silent – giving up the effort to keep up with her. So silent that the muscles of his face went into a dance, twitching and jerking, his eyes shifted crazily around the room, looking at the drapes, the ceiling, the floor.

And like that I knew that his fatigue had nothing to do with work but with something else – something more frightful than I wanted to know. If only he would open up his mouth and talk loud, brag, top her brightness, fill the room with himself. But he remained silent – and the room became steeped in his silence despite Mother's brittle brightness, her witty remarks, her deliberately brilliant face.

'Calvin,' she mocked. 'You must have a report for me. That's why I called you.'

'Report?' He answered evasively.

'Yes, report. You were supposed to go to my doctor today. Oh, don't ask me how I know. Just let us say it came to me.' She laughed shrilly. 'Or didn't you go? Perhaps you were afraid? You didn't want to hear what he would tell you?'

Calvin's eyelids quivered, quivered, kept quivering. He was not a man of softness. Gentleness came hard to him. Tenderness embarrassed him. Loving words were painful. Now he gave up any attempt at softness, and with his decision his face ceased its quivering. 'What do you want me to say,' he spoke bluntly. 'Yes, I went to the doctor. *He* wanted to see me.'

'And?'

'And – and what? I – I – I . . .' Then his voice was no longer blunt. A savage cry came out of his throat. 'You, know me, Ramona. I play the fool sometimes. I make things big – bigger than they are sometimes. But I never lie unless I can make a lie come true! Ramona, I can never lie to you!'

The room shuddered from the cry. He wanted now to fall, to hold on to something for support, instead he bit down hard so that the skin rippled over his jaws. Everything in the room followed the same contortions. The air charged electrified wavelengths, the room writhed in agony.

Mother and Calvin stood staring through each other's eyes, no longer fencing – but searching, understanding now. And as she stared, the thinness of her nostrils quivered.

'Mother!' I cried out. The cruelty of the moment had pierced us deeply. Ruby and me. But they were not aware of us. Yet I had to bring things back to normal for us, for Ruby, for me. 'Mother.' She looked at me then as though I were a stranger. 'My friend,' I pushed on desperately. 'My new friend said that her mother said you are the most beautiful woman she has ever seen.' The words, once uttered, ricocheted around the walls of the silent room, stupid, useless. 'Yes, she did,' I kept on nevertheless. 'And I felt so proud . . .'

'Proud? Proud indeed!' I recoiled from the venom of her attack. 'It is a trick! This thing beauty they talk about. Believe me, it is a low trick put out by God self.' Her face was flushed with anger. 'He puts meaning into beauty, then reduces the meaning to nothing.

'Listen to them, Calvin. Look at them flowering out into the world. Beauties both. Developing in the right

places. For what? So that the treadmill of life can un-
ravel them to suit its purpose.

'Calvin, they must take their lesson from us. From
you and me. This lesson – of how life twists us so that
we put worthless values in worthless things. Puts beauty
before you to blind you to what beauty really is. Gives
soul, then makes it sinful to have soul.

'Learn, children, learn. Or by the time you learn that
beauty is just a shell to hide behind, He reaches out and
destroys even that shell leaving you with nothing. Do
you hear? Do you see? Nothing!' She grabbed the top
of her dress and at the word 'see' she had pulled at it.
'See what life does to you when it is done tricking you
and plans to push you aside.' Ripping the dress down to
the waist with one pull, a fullness of cloth that had been
the fullness of her bosom fell to the floor at her feet,
leaving in its place a map of scars where her left breast
had been.

'Ramona, oh God, Ramona!' Calvin reached for her,
pulled her into his arms, tried to restore the torn fabric
over her bosom, and in that way to keep *their* secret
hidden from us. But Mother wrenched herself out of his
grasp, ran down the hall to her sewing room, slammed
the door, leaving us securely on the outside.

We were quiet in the living room, the three of us.
Quiet and looking furtively into each other's pain – not
directly, we could not bear that – but through the lifeless
things that meant life together and Mother: the drapes,
Mother's doodads on the coffee table, the red mohair
couch, the wall-to-wall carpet, all things reduced to in-
significance.

Even Calvin seemed not big and awesome now,

standing, a helpless part of our agony. It would have been good to go to him, to touch him, gain a little comfort by cementing our nothingness in this crisis. I did not go, perhaps from my habitual fear of him, and in another second it was too late. For throwing a glance around the room he said to no one in particular, 'I gone.' And he left us, Ruby and me, with the burden burning in our shifting eyes, of the memory of the scars that crisscrossed like roots where a breast had been. More painful because of the terrible contrast with the other breast, which was so firmly moulded into the unmarred satin of her skin that it had to be etched in both our minds as beauty's standard.

12

I often thought about Edith.

But Calvin's orders that we come directly home from school to be with Mother were strictly obeyed and I did not get any time to see Edith. Much of my time was taken up with studies with Marian. Then there was this new boy who moved to our block.

He liked me. I knew it. Every time on our way from school when we saw him, he gave me the eye. But Marian swore that she was the one he flirted with. Then one day, as we were approaching his stoop, he deliberately placed himself on the side of the sidewalk nearest me. As we walked by he breathed down the back of my neck, 'Hey baby. You sure are a fine chick.'

His breath made me tingle down my spine, all the way to the soles of my feet. I pretended not to hear him. But I did, and Marian did too. She was furious. Her birdlike eyes just didn't blink, and she pressed in her lips tight.

Delicious little bubbles of laughter fought to burst out of my mouth. I didn't want to hurt her feelings, so I swallowed hard. But my mind went on a rampage. He likes me! He likes me!

When we were out of his hearing, Marian said, 'He looks fine from a distance, but he's not so hot when you get right up on him.'

It was one thing to suppress my satisfaction. It was

another thing to kill it. 'What?' I pretended to be shocked. 'Why, I think he is the handsomest boy I ever saw. He reminds me of Jimmy Brown.' What nerve! After all of her talking I had to put up with!

Marian did not answer. Without another word to me she stomped over to her side of the street. It had been our custom to part at my stoop. I refused to let her get off that easy. 'See you tomorrow, Marian,' I called sweetly. She never turned around.

Rushing up the stairs two at a time, I flew into the apartment and into the bedroom, where in front of the long closet mirror I began a detailed examination of myself. Pulling my dress back to outline my figure, I suppressed a squeal of delight as I noticed that my breasts had grown to the size of two peaches. My calves had also thickened – at least I thought they had. I simply had to start bushing my hair out in an *au naturel*, instead of wearing the silly rat-tailed braid pinned up on my head. That was the only way my hair would seem as thick as Ruby's or, for that matter, even Marian's.

Out in the hall, I stood for a moment staring at the closed door of the back room, wondering if Mother would notice all of the changes in me. Instead I went into the living room.

'Ruby!' I cried.

'What?' Sitting on the couch, Ruby was manicuring her nails. She didn't even look up.

'Guess what!'

'Guess what about what? If you have something to tell me, go ahead. Why do I have to guess.'

My spirits refused to be dampened. 'A boy downstairs tried to get fresh with me.'

'He did wh – at?' Ruby looked up, incredulous.

'You ought to see him. He's so handsome. He lives right down the block.'

'And he got fresh with you?'

'Yes. Marian and I were . . .'

'Oh! Marian was with you.'

'Yes, but it was me he was talking to. All the other times Marian made out that she was the one. But today he showed her.'

'What did he say?'

'He said, "Hey baby," and then he said, "my, but you fine." Just like that.'

Ruby looked me up and down and then queried, 'To you?' I nodded. Waving her hand in a gesture that might have been meant to dry her fingernails as well as one to dismiss the topic, she said, 'Well, just you be careful. You know these New York boys. They don't care *who* they pick up as long as they think they can do rudeness.'

Ruby and Marian! If a boy looked at *them*, it was because they were the answer to glamour ads. But if it was *me*, the boy had to be thinking of rape! They knew what they could do to themselves! Skipping back to my room, I determined that they would never spoil my good disposition.

Nevertheless when I went back into the bedroom I sat on the bed sulking. A lot of people thought that I was good-looking. Edith did. And so did all of her sisters. Right then and there I thought of sneaking out to go to Edith's. With Mother locked up behind and Ruby making herself up in front, they would never know that I was gone. But then it would be just my luck for Mother to come out and ask for me, or for Calvin to come home the moment I left. I could wait until tomorrow. Tonight, at dinner, I would simply announce that tomorrow after school I would have to go to the library. That way no one would think of stopping or questioning me when I left the house.

But the next day when I came home from school, Ruby met me at the door. 'Didn't Mother meet you at school?' she asked.

'Why should Mother meet me at school?'

'She is not here,' Ruby whispered fearfully. 'I came home from school early. She was in the back room. Then I went into our room and started to clean up. It got so quiet in that house that I went to look again. She wasn't there.'

'Maybe she went out for a walk.'

'But why didn't she tell me?'

'You fuss too much.'

'But Daddy told us not to let her out of our sight.'

'She's out of our sight when we go to school.'

'Oh Phyllisia, why can't you understand anything? Mother might be out sick somewhere.'

'Or she might just be visiting somebody.'

'Like whom?'

That was true. Mother never visited. 'She'll be back soon,' I comforted.

'Suppose she had to be taken to a hospital.' Ruby began to cry. 'It would be all my fault.'

'How so,' I said defensively. 'After all, Mother is a big woman.'

'But Daddy told me to look after her. Do you think we should call him?'

'Are you mad?' I could see Calvin foaming and frothing at the mouth just because Mother went out without us knowing. 'He will kill us. Just let's wait a while and she'll be back.'

But although we waited hours she did not come home. As the sun began to set, Ruby wailed: 'We just can't sit around here and wait.'

I, too, had begun to worry. But I did not want to call Calvin. 'Why don't we call Mr Charles. Maybe he will take us to look for her in his car.'

At this suggestion Ruby's eyes brightened and we searched around for Mr Charles' number, which we finally found in the telephone book. But when we called, he was not at home. Next we called Cousin Frank.

'But he doesn't have a car,' Ruby said.

'He knows where Mr Charles is,' I answered. 'Like Mutt and Jeff they never are too long parted.' Within the hour Mr Charles and Cousin Frank were ringing our doorbell.

'What time did you say she went out?' Mr Charles asked.

'It was about two o'clock. I came home early and began to clean up my room . . .'

'After all,' Cousin Frank bit deeply down at the side of his mouth holding his cigar, 'a woman can come and go as she well please without having to give an account to her children.'

All of the lines of Mr Charles' massive face had deepened with concern. Even his fingers drumming the arms of his chair showed his restlessness. Yet he calmly said: 'It is only seven now. It would be different if it was midnight.'

104

'But Mother just doesn't go out,' Ruby insisted. 'She wasn't feeling well.'

'What to do, Frank? Take the car and go look for her?'

'Where in this big city? I would suggest that we simply call Calvin.'

'No!' I had not meant to shout. Moderating my voice, I pleaded. 'Don't tell Daddy. He will kill us.'

'Chuu – pps,' Mr Charles sucked his back teeth. 'Calvin ain't killing nobody.'

The cigar in Cousin Frank's mouth trembled a little. 'The big crime of his life is that he make you two children afraid to talk to him. It ain't only a shame, it is also a sin.'

And he reached for the telephone, but luckily at that moment Mother came in. The two men rushed to her as she stood in the doorway. Mr Charles put his great arms around her shoulders. She collapsed against him and he picked her up, brought her into the room and laid her on the couch. 'Ramona, Ramona. What is it? Tell me, what is it?' They hovered over her like two hens, rubbing her hands, her feet.

We seemed not to belong, Ruby and I, to that scene unfolding before us. I had no thought except a strange wish that had nothing to do with what we were looking at. I wished that I was across the ocean on The Island.

It was a long time before Mother opened her eyes and looked at her two friends. 'Frank – Charles, I am tired. Oh, I'm so very, very tired.'

13

I needed Edith.

I needed a friend who understood what I was going through. Edith had had this experience, so she was that friend. As simple as that.

I had not seen Edith since before school started – over two months. But things had become hair-raisingly difficult at home. Ruby and I had to take turns staying home with Mother, and while Ruby loved to stay with her, I hated it. How to explain this to just anyone?

Mother was not simply tired – she had given up. She no longer changed from depressive moods to sparkling bright moods. She had moved to a world beyond all of that, a world beyond us. Strangely enough, Ruby did not seem to notice. Ruby enjoyed fussing over people, and fussing over Mother kept her in a continual state of bliss: She combed Mother's hair, prepared special meals, even stitched up nightgowns to match, in colour, the blankets that we used to wrap Mother in when she sat in the living room.

I, on the other hand, never knew what to do. Remembering how she spoke about my love of books, I read to her – even though I knew she never heard a word. She was always so occupied with her other world. Once I started, I could not stop. I read until Mother's impersonal stare left those scary, unknown places to look somewhere over my shoulder, questioning an unseen person about why this girl troubled herself when she had no desire to be disturbed.

I felt that other person behind me, touching me lightly, and I tingled from my bristling hair all the way down my spine. Looking around quickly, I saw no one, but upon turning back, found Mother smiling at me – suggesting that *we* shared the secret of that unknown person. My hair stood on end, my scalp crawled and pores stood up all over me. So it wasn't surprising when I started out one morning by rushing out to get someone to stay with me – namely Edith.

Calvin and Ruby were safely on their way when I made this dash to Edith's house. But she was not at home. Randy told me where to find her, and I took a bus all the way down to the lower part of Harlem. The employment agency that I entered had a sign outside written in bold letters: HOUSEWORK. MAIDS, DAY'S WORK, CHAUFFEURS.

Edith was sitting in a row of folding chairs, along with many grownups. She was chewing gum and gazing around in an offhand way. I signalled her from the door. She did not recognize me at first.

'Hey, Phyl, how ya doin'?' She jumped to her feet and manoeuvered past the extended knees to get to me. 'What you doing here, girl? Come to see me?' I nodded and we stood grinning at each other. 'Girl, I ain't seen you in so long. I thought you had done give me up.'

'Oh, silly.'

Edith had changed. It seemed that the shadow that had always hovered over her had settled. She no longer looked young. 'What's happenin',' she asked 'no school today?'

'Do *you* have to work today?' I answered her question with one of my own.

'Me? I got to work every day. We just here waiting for a call.'

'A call?'

'Yeah, for some folks – mostly white folks – who need a day's work done.'

'Oh – I wanted you to come home with me.'

Edith hesitated. But only for an instant. 'If you want me . . .' Then shrugging. 'I didn't feel like working anyway.'

I sighed in relief that she was still young in this way. But then I had never really doubted that she would agree to come with me. After all, she was my best friend.

We took the bus, and as we settled in our seats, Edith asked: 'Things tough at home, huh?' I nodded. 'You mother?' I nodded again. It was so good to have an understanding friend like Edith.

Yet I found that as much as I appreciated her, was glad to see her, I was still uncomfortable sitting next to her on the bus. It had been a long time since I had seen her and I had forgotten how shabby she looked. I kept telling myself that perhaps it was because I was dressed so much more differently – better – than before. Or maybe it was because I was used to being with Marian these days. But then of course the reason I had never invited Edith home was because she *was* so shabby.

Old thoughts of Calvin's anger rushed to me and I wondered if I had done a wise thing by asking her home. On the street I tried to put a distance between us as we walked, aware of her worn coat, her turned-over shoes.

My face flushed hot and then cold as I imagined that passers-by would identify me with Edith.

Not noticing my discomfort, Edith asked: 'How does it feel going to high school?'

'Great,' I answered keeping my head straight, my eyes away from her. 'It's hard as hell though. All of the kids from our old school are having a tough time. Lots of them are dropping out. The work is too hard.'

'Only for them?'

'Mostly for them and the kids from the schools around Harlem. You know how they never taught us anything. Then to have to jump from algebra that we never learned to geometry is nothing to play with. Lucky thing I have a sister to help me.'

'You always was lucky.' Edith's tone was wistful. I looked at her, but there was no trace of resentment in her face. After a few seconds she said: 'One thing though, you sure look ba-a-ad, since you started going to that school, really gone.'

Blushing with pleasure, I slackened my pace to fall in step with her. 'Oh well, you know how it is. *All* the girls dress up to go to *that* school.'

We were passing a drugstore and Edith left me to go in. Waiting outside, I mused that, after all, it had been lucky that Edith did not go to my school. I wondered if I would have been still 'best friends' with her if she had. I flushed guiltily. Certainly she would always be a better friend than Marian.

Mother was already in the living room, sitting on the rocker that Calvin had bought, when we came in. Guilty, because I had not been there to help her, I began talking the moment I entered. 'Mother, guess what? I brought my friend to see you. Her name is Edith.'

'Hello, Miss Cathy,' Edith smiled and the dimples deepening at the sides of her mouth made her look almost her old self.

'Ahh, you are the little girl who sent me those lovely flowers this summer.'

'What?' I had almost forgotten. 'Oh yes. She is the one.'

'I brought another little present that I picked up on the way.' Edith pulled an unwrapped bottle of perfume from her coat.

Picked it up indeed, I thought resentfully, realizing the reason she had stopped at the drugstore. Masking my annoyance, I said pleasantly, 'Why don't you rest your coat, Edith.' She struggled out of her coat, and folding it to hide the torn lining, I placed it on the back of the couch.

Expectantly, I waited for her to make some comment about the house, the furnishings in the living room – the red couch that looked so elegant to me, the drapes, cleaned and rehung for the coming holidays – but Edith sitting on a stool at Mother's feet seemed not to notice the glaring contrast of my home to that dark railroad flat where she lived.

Instead, she looked steadily at Mother. 'Phyl told me you were beautiful,' she said at last. 'But she never told me *how* beautiful.' Edith's charm in getting past ordinary obstacles of politeness immediately began to melt the oppressiveness of the apartment. It ought to have melted my resentment too. That was why I had brought her. But it didn't. How dared she sit there pretending she was not impressed by her surroundings!

'You are a charming child,' Mother smiled. 'I knew

you would be. I did so want Phyllisia to bring you to meet me. But it seemed that you were always busy.'

Not by a blink or pause did Edith betray me. Yet she must have remembered that I had never even mentioned to her the possibility that she might visit me. 'Well you know how it is, Miss Cathy. I got so much to do with all those kids and stuff.'

'Kids?'

'Sure, all my sisters. I got four of them, and a brother. By the time I get finished messing with them I ain't got time to go nowhere.' She then went into a detailed description of all the things she had to do, and how Randy never helped her. She talked rapidly, taking seriously the business of keeping the apartment lively. She made serious things appear funny so that Mother laughed. I did not laugh. My annoyance over her calm, relaxed manner kept mounting. It was as though she was used to being around people like Mother.

'But tell me,' Mother said during a pause in the conversation. 'You don't go to school?' Too late we realized that she had been looking beyond Edith's words, prying open the door of our secret. 'I don't hear you talk about your mother, your father. Where are they?' We both stared at her, tongue-tied. 'You don't have parents?'

Ruby came in at that moment, giving us no time to answer. 'Mother,' she gushed into the living room. 'I just couldn't stay in school today thinking something was happening to you. And besides, I don't think I should go to school any more until you get better.' Then she saw Edith. 'Oh, you have company? How nice.'

'Yes, Phyllisia brought her friend home to charm me and she is doing a good job of it.'

'I'm so glad,' she said and went to take off her coat.

Ruby's pleasure seemed genuine. Perhaps she had not noticed Edith's clothes. On the little stool where she sat, Edith was half-hidden by the coffee table. I waited for Ruby to come back. I knew she would say something about Edith's clothes and I carefully planned my rebuke. But when Ruby bounced back into the living room she went to sit on the floor next to Edith's stool. I knew I should have been pleased. But I wasn't. It was as though I was the only one who noticed how untidy Edith was.

'What's your name?' Ruby asked.

'Edith.'

'My name is Ruby.'

'Yes, I know.' Edith's voice was hushed, her eyes wide with admiration. 'Phyl told a lot about you.'

Warming under the bright glow of Edith's stare, Ruby lowered her long, sooty eyelashes as though playing to a gallery of boys. 'Oh, does Phyllisia talk about me? Tell me what my little sister says.' Ruby didn't care who it was, as long as she had admirers. That's why she pretended not to notice Edith's clothes.

'She always say the nicest things about you,' Edith lied. 'She told me about how glamorous you are.'

'My sister?' Ruby turned her wide smile to me. My anger mounted. I had told Edith that Ruby was glamorous, but not in that way. Everyone in the room seemed to be acting out lies. I certainly was not going to join them.

'You know,' Ruby said to Edith. 'I saw you before. One day last summer a friend of mine and I went for a walk in the park, and I saw you and Phyllisia and some other little kids playing.'

'How come you didn't come over and talk,' Edith inquired.

'Oh we had so much to talk about,' Ruby answered. 'And besides, you know how secretive Phyllisia is about everything. She never *wanted* us to know where she was hanging out, so I thought I would just let her think she still had her secret.'

It was hard to keep sitting, pretending that I was enjoying the conversation. Ruby had known about Edith and had said nothing to me about it. She had some nerve! Spying on me! Then the other thought occurred to me. Hadn't she seen anything *wrong* with my being with *Edith*? Wrong enough to at least tell Mother or perhaps even Calvin?

'I wish you *had* come and talked to us,' Edith sounded regretful. 'My sisters sure would have been turned on. They're crazy about Phyl. They think that she's so pretty. They'd have thought the same about you.'

'Phyllisia pretty?' Ruby laughed. Then looking me over half-teasingly she said, 'Well, I guess high school *has* brought her out a little. Don't you think so, Mother? At least, looking at her now, nobody would think that just a couple of years ago she was nothing but a barefoot little girl running around her aunt's backyard.'

Jumping to my feet I stood towering over Ruby. 'How dare you sit there and tell such a damn lie! I never went barefoot in my life!' The force of my anger surprised them. I had never sworn before Mother.

Ruby was silent for a moment, then she gave a little surprised laugh and said calmly, 'What are you talking about Phyllisia? You *know* that we always ran around barefoot at home.'

I saw my world crumbling – not only did they sit here as though they accepted Edith as one of them but now they were deliberately tearing down my life on the Island to please Edith. 'I'm not going to have you sit there telling lies on me,' I shouted. 'I'm not! The next thing you will be saying is that we were poor and dirty and went around with socks full of holes and runover shoes! You'll be saying that we were dirty, nasty little orphan brats with no one to look after us.'

I was shouting down at Ruby, but my words were directed at Edith. And Edith knew. I felt her start, felt her surprised stare attach itself to the side of my face, big round dark eyes, burning the side of my face. I wanted to stop but I couldn't. My anger doubled and I kept shouting.

Ruby remained calm. 'We were poor,' she said, looking into my impassioned face. 'I don't know about all the rest of the things you were talking about. But the reason our shoes didn't run over was because Auntie never let us wear them after school and we went barefoot, barefoot, barefoot.'

The force of my slap snapped her head back. It was a stunning blow, but so unexpected that even Ruby did not fully realize she had been hit. It came to her slowly, and when it did, she jumped up reaching for my hair with both hands.

'What's going on here? I say what the hell is going on here?' We had not heard him come in, but suddenly Calvin stood in the doorway like some terrible monster, shocked, incredulous. 'What kind of noise you making here in front of my wife – in front of your mother?' He was in a rage.

Ruby and I stood panting into each other's face, waiting for his wrath to descend. He reached out, grabbed each of us by an arm, pulled us almost off the floor. Then he saw Edith.

'What she doing here?' His words strangled him. No one answered. 'I ask what in the hell is this little ragamuffin doing in my house?'

Ruby came to Edith's defence. 'She's a friend of Phyllisia's. She came to see Mother.'

'Tell she get out!'

'But Daddy,' Ruby protested. 'Look at this lovely present she brought for Mother.'

'Tell she to take it and get out. I'll give you ten seconds.'

'Mother,' Ruby pleaded. But Mother had slipped back into her world. She wanted no part of rows and anger.

'That's why I'm running in bad luck,' he fumed. 'Because of these picky-headed ragamuffins you got breathing down me tail. Get she out!'

His anger satisfied me. He would get Edith straight. She would know that I was no barefoot girl, had never been a barefoot girl running around anybody's yard. What nerve! Sitting in here as though she belonged and taking sides with Ruby against me. He would show her!

Ruby looked into my face and stilled another protest. Edith reached for her coat. She held it and did not leave, not right away. She waited, waited with a hurt trembling in place of her dimples at the corners of her mouth. She

115

waited for just one look – one look that would say that I had not been talking to her, about her, that I did not mean to act the way I had acted, that I was not that kind of person.

I never looked at her. Yet every one of my pores saw her, heard her, felt her as she struggled into her coat. They followed her movements as she walked silently to the door, as she stood one final moment waiting, waiting.

Silence hung heavily in the room when she had gone. No one broke it, not even Calvin. Perhaps he was now ashamed – of himself, of me. But I was not!

Clinging stubbornly to my anger, I looked around the room, then biting down on my jaws so that the skin rippled over them, I stalked out of the living room and down the hall into my bedroom, slammed the door, threw myself across the bed and lay there, shaking in every limb.

I lay there for a long time, until gradually the shaking ceased. I heard Calvin pass the door on the way to his room. I heard when he walked back to the front. Mother called him, 'Calvin, have you lost your humanity? How could you treat a poor girl so?'

'I ain't know what you talking,' he mumbled. 'The one thing I know is I don't want people looking that way in this house. They don't go with the furniture.'

'You have come a long way since my father would use those same words to you. "You don't go with my furniture."'

'Ramona, I living in the present, not the past. When history advance, it is current events. And I ain't need no past in the present to bring me bad luck.' He slammed out of the house, and once again a strange quiet fell over the apartment.

They did not disturb me. They left me with my anger. And I held on to it. They did not understand. I had been right. I had been right. Yet when I tried to piece what had actually happened together, nothing really made sense. I only knew that I had somehow been defending some precious truth about myself – about them, and no one seemed to appreciate it. But time slipped by, and it became more and more difficult to hold on to my anger.

Suddenly waves and waves of shame burned me from the top of my head to the tip of my toes. I did not want to think nor look at anyone – not Ruby, not Mother, not myself, and never, never again Edith. I pulled myself into a ball on the bed, letting the waves take me and push me about. And still no one disturbed me.

The house had long resumed its customary sounds. Ruby's footsteps walked efficiently from kitchen to living room. It was my day to prepare dinner, but she never called me. The day rushed into the early evening of late fall. Dinner dishes rattled on the tray as Ruby walked past the door. Why didn't she call me? It wasn't like Ruby to ignore me. Suddenly I had the answer – Mother had prevented her.

14

I had fallen into a deep, dream-ravaged sleep when Ruby, preparing to go to bed, awakened me. 'Mother wants to see you,' she said. I searched her face for a clue of what might be in store for me. But Ruby's face gave no answers. 'She is in bed.'

Going to face Mother was my great punishment. Everything about me was heavy with guilt. My head refused to sit straight on my neck, my eyelids pressed my eyes towards the floor, and my legs had weights making them difficult to be moved. I wanted only one thing: that the floor would open up and suck me down to the darkest of places.

'I am not going to scold you,' Mother said. My head hung even lower. I wanted her to scold me. I deserved to be scolded, beaten, stomped to the ground. 'But I want to talk to you, for we have never really talked to each other.'

Why should she want to talk to me in life? I had proven myself such a horror. 'Let us clear the air by saying that we both are very unhappy about what happened today. We both are very, very ashamed. I want to take my share of the blame for what happened to that lovely Edith. I *am* as much to blame as anyone.'

No, how could she say that! She had been so nice to Edith. Even Ruby had been nice. I was the one to blame. Me!

'I don't know what reasons you gave yourself for the way you behaved. You were so upset from the moment she sat down.' She waited for me to answer. But what could I answer? I didn't know.

'Phyllisia – she called you Phyl, didn't she? I like the name. You see, Phyl, grownups are very strange people. They have a habit of seeing everything in terms of themselves – *their* problems. It is always the rent *we* have to pay, the food *we* have to buy, the clothes *we* have to wear, the children *we* must care for. You see, *our* problems.

'It is hard, no matter how we try, to think of our children as outside of us, with problems of their own. So naturally it is difficult to guide them.

'If I had not been so caught up with all of my problems – my – my – fears – I might have been able to see some of the things happening about me. I would have known – should have known – what *you* were going through. Sometimes I was so glad for you and Ruby to leave the house, leave me alone with my problems. That's why I never really insisted that you bring home your friends. That's why I never allowed myself to see that, living in the same house with such a person as your father, it was natural that you copy some of his ways.'

Copy Calvin's ways! Never! I was stung by the remark, but I could not forget my satisfaction over his treatment of Edith.

'I am not condemning your father. He is the way he is. I love him the way he is. I wouldn't have wanted him any other way. And because of that, today was the first time I allowed myself to see that the things we love and accept, the things we value, make us parents *our children's* problems.'

She smoothed out the edge of the bed and drew me down beside her. 'That's why I too am to blame. But then perhaps the only reason I see it now is that for me the emphasis of things has changed. Things that were right and things that were wrong, or what I considered right and wrong, have lost their distinction. Now, what I considered right is completely wrong, and what a short time ago I might have considered wrong, is just the way of things.'

Her voice broke off but she struggled on. 'I grew up with the words of the Bible ringing in my ears: "Children, obey thy parents, so that thy life may be longer on this earth . . ." But after today my plea must be: "Children, by all means, by whatever means, change your parents so that the lives of all of us – all of the Ediths – must be more bearable on this earth."

'But then you see, Phyl, I am going to die!' I sickened before the force of those words. I think that I had known it, that I had already accepted it. But to hear her *say* it, 'I am going to die,' forced me to fight against my knowledge and to fight against her acceptance of it. But she held my hands firmly as I tried to move away. Held me while her eyes moved from object to object, around the room. 'Yes, I am going to die – and oh my God Phyllisia, it is so hard to die. Of all the things in the world, this surely must be the hardest.'

Why was she saying this to me? I didn't want to listen. I tried again to escape her grasp, but she held on.

'You know, Phyl,' she said. 'It puts one in the mind of Christmas. That yearly event that children all over the Christian world await so anxiously. Tense, excited, uncertain, will it never come? Then suddenly it is Christ-

120

mas Eve and they realize that after all it has come too quickly. Nothing they can do can prevent tomorrow from being Christmas Day. Then in one brief day it is over – over. The day after, Christmas is only a memory.

'And so we wait for *that* day that we know must come, realizing that the day following *we* will be just a memory. It is not easy. Of all the things that we must live through, this surely must be the hardest . . .'

Her voice faltered and the thinness of her nostrils quivered. She held up a hand to the lamp at the side of the bed, and we both watched, fascinated, the outlines of her bones through the pale, translucent skin. 'They were strong once. I used to branch from tree to tree on The Island, right along with the boys. You didn't know that, did you? I used to climb and swim and even fight. I thought of no one but myself. Spending my years towards adulthood as a fool spends money. That was not long ago, but that too is a memory.'

She looked at me then. 'Ah Phyllisia – Phyl, I am making it hard for you, yes? But what am I to do? Should I simply have scolded you, let you unburden your guilt and say to me you are sorry. To *me!* You might have felt better but what of responsibility? Mine to you – yours to yourself – to people? I waited too long. I have no time left and so I must be cruel. You *must* not forget this day – what you have done today – easily. I want it so. Guilt carries its own sickness, but it also carries its own cure. But a memory can do nothing that will stand up against time and experience.'

15

She was dead!

They said she was. But I did not believe it. I felt her presence sitting quietly in the living room. I heard her footsteps walking silently down the hall, and when I prepared food in the kitchen, she kept her constant vigil over my shoulder. Yet the strangers said she was dead and kept coming into our house, some claiming a vague sort of friendship, others saying they were relatives – they kept coming like roaches out of woodwork.

The men sat in the back room, her sewing room, where she had spent so many hours of so many days, sewing or looking out of the garbage-piled backyard where alley cats screeched and bits of hardy grass inevitably grew between the cracks in the concrete. The women sat smugly in the living room, clucking their tongues, scratching at details like chickens pecking in stubborn soil for loose ends to chew into meaty gossip. A lifetime of envy, spanning the ocean, from The Island to New York, would go to add to the flavour.

In the trancelike state between dream and reality where I moved, I caught snatches of their conversation, 'Yes my dear, she always did want to be alone. Well she alone now, hope she enjoy it.' 'The restaurant, huh? Someone will enjoy it. I wonder who?' 'Wall-to-wall carpeting, huh? Class, my dear. Pity you can't take it with you.' 'Calvin will get lonely – well we shall see my dear. We shall see . . .' The level of their sorrow remained at pointing with I-told-you-so eyes and a rapid exchange of digging elbows into each other's ribs.

No, there was not enough sorrow in the house – her house. Not enough tears. The walls did not pour down tears, the doodads on the coffee table kept their material indifference and the mohair couch remained a determined red – all allies of the strangers who sat complacently, scrutinizing all.

Ruby did not cry. She had no tears left. Calvin did not cry. He walked from room to room, his light-brown eyes questioning the furniture, the drapes, the much talked about wall-to-wall carpeting. They also questioned me, and Ruby. Where is she? Where is she? Where the hell is she? they asked. For, like me, he did not believe – refused to believe – that she was dead.

Neither did I cry. My tears balled into one huge fist that settled painfully in my throat, refusing to flow, allowing no food to pass, no words to pass. They said that I was grieving, those strangers. They said that I was grieving to my death. You must cry, they commanded. You must eat a little, drink a little, and cry. But I looked into their smug, complacent faces, their greedy eyes, their vulturelike beaks, and the ball in my throat only thickened.

Dry-eyed, I stood at the window, my back deliberately closing them out along with the room, and looked at pedestrians bending against the sharp wind that whipped snow into whirlpools, flung it into resisting faces and against windows with the sound of glass cracking against glass. Snow had fallen on snow, creating high mountains of covered ice that busy people walked around and children climbed over in their everlasting need to do something, get somewhere.

It was dark in the limousine that picked us up at the house to take us to the funeral parlour. That was the way it should be – the way the world should be – dark and in mourning. We were together in the car, Calvin and Ruby and I, and that too was the way it should be, together the grievers. During the funeral service the strangers would gather again. And later back at the house, for the wake, those same strangers would come to drink and laugh and gossip again, for no one should sleep until after the burial tomorrow. But for one moment, we who cared were together. Calvin sat next to the driver, his head thoughtfully, quietly bent. Ruby and I sat in the back, clinging to each other – close – closer than we had ever been. Out on the streets, pedestrians scurried before the efforts of the cold, biting wind. And that too was justice, that the wind wiped laughter from the faces and the mouths of people.

Outside of the funeral home a small crowd had gathered, and as the car pulled up, tense whispers rose like vapour. 'Here's the family.' 'Who they?' 'Dunno, hear tell he the one who owns that restaurant – you know the one . . .' 'Dunno.'

The curious and the sorrow seekers, wanting to look at and touch and feel sadness – to pity. 'What a shame. I seen her. Young! Pretty too.' Looking, crowding, pushing to see. 'That her husband? Sure is fine.' '. . . children – poor motherless things . . .' We followed Calvin up the entrance, waited while the funeral director cleared a path.

In the dim light of the street with the muddled faces

of the curious as background, one girl pushed her oldish-young face up to mine, black eyes, distinct and tear-streaked, 'Phyl. Phyl, I'm sorry. I'm so sorry. What can I do? I'll do anything – anything . . .'

But Mr Charles had joined Calvin, together they entered the funeral parlour and Ruby and I had to follow. We were led directly up to the open casket, stood looking down at a stranger with her beauty fixed on her face. Black hair, soft and wavy, nestled luxuriously on white satin cushions, eyes that were never going to see again, obviously forced shut, lips turned up into a smile that had never been *her* smile. A beautiful stranger, but a stranger nevertheless. A wax artist must have formed that nose that would never again quiver at the thinness of its nostrils.

'I shall not remember her like this,' Ruby vowed. And as though those were the only words needed, her tears once more began to flow. 'Oh I swear, Phyllisia, I shall never remember her like this.'

And how shall I remember? I saw her lying in bed, her hand held up to the light, I heard her voice whisper in my ear as I heard it every night, 'I spent my youth as a fool spends money . . .' I turned quickly, but as usual no one was there.

Sitting next to Ruby, staring at the casket, at the outline of her face raised above the opening, at the flowers laid in abundance to decorate the casket – white flowers, pink flowers, blue flowers, stifling the room with the hideousness of finality – I heard the voice again in my ear, '. . . but you see Phyl, I am going to die!' The hairs of my head bristled, and I tensed, thinking to get up and run.

But at that moment a streak of red rushed down the

aisle and posed starkly among the delicate flowers. A woman, a familiar woman, a tenant in our house wearing a red coat. She gazed down at the face in the opening, then looked at Calvin, next she searched Ruby's face, and finally her eyes rested on mine. Breaking off a flower from one of the wreaths, she darted up to me, pushing the flower into my hand. I yanked my hands away, then sat gaping at the flower that had fallen to the floor, a lily, white and waxed, looking like death itself.

'Don't sit there holding it in, child,' the woman pleaded. 'Cry! It is the dead that we cry for, not the living. When He takes a person's life, He takes away all they got. Sure we don't starve no more and we don't hurt no more and we don't have no more worry. But then there ain't no more planning and no more feeling and no more laughing and loving either. So cry, child, cry that He done took life away.' Then rushing up the aisle she disappeared as quickly as she had appeared.

'I am the darkness and the light. Those who believe in me though they are dead so shall they live.' And the voice whispered in my ear in contradiction, 'Oh my God, it is so hard to die . . .' Ruby clutched my arm and I held her hand tightly.

'Yea, though I walk in the shadow of darkness, I will fear no evil,' the preacher intoned.

And the voice said, '. . . of all the things in the world this must be the hardest . . .' I wove my fingers through Ruby's, squeezing hers.

Preacher: 'You are with me.'

Voice: '. . . it puts you in the mind of Christmas . . .'

Preacher: 'Thy rod and thy staff, they comfort me.'

'Ramona, Ramona.' Calvin's voice loud and braying

126

like a donkey's filled the room. He rushed to the casket and threw himself over the opening. Bewildered, I saw Mr Charles go to him, put his arms around his shoulders and lead him to a side room. Why had Mr Charles taken Calvin away?

Voice: '. . . he is the way he is. I love him the way he is . . .' I leaned heavily against Ruby.

Preacher, clearing his throat: 'I have a most unusual request. I am used to preaching a sermon for the souls of the dearly departed. But Mr Cathy has given me to understand that I knew too little about the late Mrs Cathy to preach a sermon or give a eulogy.'

One of the strangers who had been in the living room whispered behind me in low sarcasm, 'I should hope so. Can you imagine a Catholic being preached over by a Baptist preacher?' A second stranger replied.

'It's beyond me. But how could Calvin bring his wife to a Baptist parlour!'

The first stranger: 'It's a shame. But you know she stopped attending Mass.'

Preacher: 'Mr Cathy insists that I only say these few words.'

First stranger: 'No m'dear, she can't even be buried on consecrated soil.'

Second stranger: 'You don't say. Imagine, a woman with her upbringing.'

Preacher: 'She was lovely. She was strong. She was good. Amen.'

A murmur of disappointment rose from all those who had saved their tears for a ringing sermon.

First stranger: 'That's all? Calvin must want the poor Baptist to drop dead.'

'Ramona, oh God, Ramona,' Calvin's sobs came out of the side room.

Voice: '. . . Calvin, but how could you treat a poor girl so . . .'

'Ramona, Ramona,' Calvin sobbed.

Preacher: 'Now if you will all rise and join me in song.' The congregation stood.

Preacher, singing: 'Rock of ages . . .'

Everyone joined in: 'Cleft for me. Let me hide myself in thee.'

Ruby screamed, collapsed. A handful of people rushed to her, led her into the side room.

Congregation singing: 'Rock of ages . . .'

Voice: '. . . I am cruel. I am cruel . . . that poor girl . . .'

Why had they taken Ruby away? They had taken Calvin and now they had taken Ruby. I was alone.

First stranger: 'Eheh, but what kind of sermon you call this? She was lovely . . .'

Second stranger: 'You know Calvin, m'dear, making style, always making style.'

Voice: '. . . What did she call you – Phyl? I like that name . . .'

Edith – where was Edith? I had seen her but where was she now? I looked wildly around the room. Everyone was sitting, and I still could not see her.

Voice: '. . . I'm a memory Phyl – only a memory . . .'

Edith! She was outside. I had seen her outside. 'Edith!' I shouted, so that she would wait for me. She had to wait for me, not leave me in this room full of strangers.

First stranger: 'But what's wrong with the girl?'

128

Second stranger: 'Must be the strain. She grieving hard – too hard.'

I struggled past knees blocking my way, ran up the aisle.

'Hold her, hold her. The child sick. Don't let her go.'

The streets were dark, empty. 'Eeeedith! Eeeedith!'

Hands came out of the pitch darkness, dozens and dozens of hands, claiming me, holding.

Scratching and clawing I tried to get away, tried to run, found myself being borne down, smothered. I was on the ground, feet all around me. A riot. Where was Edith to save me?

'Come, child, come. Don't carry on so. You mustn't shame your mother's memory so.'

What stranger was this talking about my mother – calling her a memory. She was not a memory – she was not . . .

'Eeeedith . . .'

Part Three

16

I had long dreams. The nightmare began the moment I closed my eyes: A pretty lady with soft, wavy, black hair braided and hanging to her waist, stepped out of the shadows and whispered to me, 'You will not forget this day easily, Phyllisia. You will not.'

'I shall. I shall.' Words leaped from my throat but could not pass through my open mouth. My teeth had grown to form bars. Words beat against my teeth, like birds protesting their cage; none could escape.

Laughing, she ran through the forest, passing through trees, teasing, repeating: 'No, no, you will not forget . . .'

Twisting and turning, clawing at my jaw with hands that I could not see – because I was sleeping – shouting with words that I could not form, my anger against my deformity changed swiftly to mortal terror. The lady was approaching a cliff and still no words escaped with which I could warn her. I knew if she fell into the roaring water, she would be torn into a million pieces by jagged rocks submerged just below.

But I was sleeping, mute, imprisoned with my caged words, gazing through the bars of my teeth. I pulled and pounded on them as she moved nearer, nearer to the cliff's edge.

'I'll tell her. I'll tell her for you.' Edith ran out of the darkness, ran up to me, then over me, pounding my prone, helpless self with her passing feet. 'I'll hurry and tell her for you.' She rushed on, but the lady had faded, and it was Edith alone dashing headlong towards that empty space.

'No, Edith, don't go. Don't go. Turn back. Turn back.' She turned, pointed to me and said: 'Yes, I'm going. You were nasty to me, I'm going.' She ran, leaving me shaking at the gates that were my teeth and screaming . . . screaming . . .

'Come, Phyllisia, get up. Get up.' Wildly I fought against the hand that was holding me, pulling me, shaking me away from Edith. I opened my eyes and I was looking into Ruby's worried face. 'It's time to eat,' she said. Placing the tray of food at the side of the bed, she propped up the pillows behind me. 'What's the matter, Phyllisia?' she asked, 'Dreaming again?' I nodded, letting her wipe the sweat of troubled sleep from my brow. 'Same thing?' I nodded again. 'If you would eat something, you'd stop dreaming. At least that's what they say.'

They – meaning the concerned strangers who had thought it their duty to give a little 'direction' to those two poor 'motherless children'. But their duty had its limitations. After one or two mercy visits, they had stopped coming, leaving only their useless advice behind them.

'I boiled fish,' Ruby coaxed. 'I put a lot of lemon on it the way you used to like it on The Island. And I mashed potatoes with a lot of butter.'

Poor Ruby worried so much about me that I would have eaten anything to please her. 'If you eat,' she promised, 'I will stay and keep you company. But if you don't, I'll leave you in the room all by yourself.'

134

If I wasn't being haunted – I would *ask* Ruby to leave me. Not that she would. Ruby had a mania for taking care of the sick. First it had been Mother and now me. She never left me alone. She fussed so much, fixing and refixing our bedroom, combing my hair, dressing me. She had insisted on walking me to the bathroom long before I had become too weak to make that trip myself. The only time I had any rest was when she would go to school – but then that was when the haunting began.

'Come,' Ruby forced a piece of fish into my mouth. I tried to swallow but gagged, brought it back up into Ruby's waiting hand. Tears of discouragement came to her eyes – Ruby cried so easily. 'O.K. I won't force you. But drink a little milk.'

Thankfully I drank a little. The doctor had said milk was keeping me alive. The spirit had stopped me from eating but it hadn't stopped me from drinking. People said that I couldn't eat because I was grieving, but I knew it was the spirit that kept haunting me. It moved around the room when I was alone. It whispered in my ear, it crept into my sleep. I was afraid, but more than afraid, puzzled. If it was who I thought it was, then why didn't it let me eat? And what about Edith? Was it trying to tell me something about Edith?

'Did anyone come to see me?' I asked Ruby after she had taken the tray into the kitchen and bustled back, ready to upset the room again. 'I mean while I was sleeping?'

'No, nobody.' But then, why should Edith come? How did she know she would not be insulted again?

'Marian said she'd be here later.' Marian? What a bore. 'I saw her on my way home.' Ruby was picking up things and putting them down in the same spot. I could never understand her method of straightening up. 'I made her promise that she would bring her homework so that we could all do it together.'

'I don't feel like it, Ruby.' It was obvious to anyone but Ruby that I was too weak to concentrate on homework.

'Don't be silly. You can't fall that far back in your schoolwork. Anyhow, Marian said she had something to tell me.'

It was no use protesting, Ruby wanted to see Marian. Most of Ruby's friends had stopped coming around because I took up so much of her time. Only Marian still came occasionally – supposedly to see me.

'There, doesn't that look better?' She looked around the room with an air of satisfaction. It looked the same. 'Now we have to freshen *you* up a bit.' She brought out comb, brush and a fresh nightgown, and I braced myself for her attention.

'That old chick thinks she's cute,' Ruby complained. 'Always coming around here showing off. But don't trouble your head. When you fill out again, you'll look ten times better than she.'

Nothing was troubling me except Ruby. Why was she fixing me up for Marian when all she could do was find fault with the girl? To hear her, one would think that Ruby didn't like Marian. 'And anyway, she's too short. Can you imagine that sawed-off runt trying to act like something?' Then slyly:

'I want to prepare you for a shock before she comes in running her big mouth.' Lowering her voice confidentially as though someone else were in the house,

'Marian's going around with that boy you like. She told me.' I really didn't care. But if I said so, Ruby would not believe me. 'She says that you used to *think* that he liked you, but that she was the one he liked all the time. I know she's lying. But that's the type she is. The minute you got sick, I bet she just went around him shaking her tail and giving him the high sign. But that's all right. We'll show her. Wait until you get some flesh on your bones.'

Tugging and pulling, brushing my hair, her voice sounded vindictive. 'Just wait until she comes in and starts her foolishness, and listen to what I'll tell her.' Ruby tied a bow in my hair – big and babyish-looking – then stood back to admire her handiwork. But thankfully the bell rang before she could change my gown.

Marian came in looking healthy: plump, brown and cheerful. Standing at the foot of my bed, she gave me a long look before she made her prepared statement, 'God, Phyllisia, but you look awful.'

Ruby rushed to my defence, 'How is she supposed to look if she's sick? If you were sick for two months, do you think you'd be looking fat and dumpy as you do?'

'It's just that every time I come here she looks worse and worse.' But after a few seconds, she decided to be nice.

'How *do* you feel, Phyllisia?'

'Sick, stupid,' Ruby retorted. 'If she was feeling well, she'd be out of bed.'

'Oh well,' Marian sat at the foot of the bed. 'Do you really *want* to do homework? I don't feel like it.'

'I thought that's what you came here for,' Ruby answered for me again. 'I was just telling Phyllisia that it was lucky that you live right up the block.'

'It sure is,' Marian agreed. Then the reason for her coming spread smugly across her face. Only Ruby had already prepared me. 'You know what, Phyllisia, Norman and I went to the movies last night. He came to my house to pick me up. My mother thinks he's the most.' I looked at her flat, birdlike eyes and thought of Edith's with their layers of darkness and interest that one could actually search through. 'You remember him, don't you, Phyllisia? Norman is the boy who was always making passes at me last term.'

I only looked at her wondering if it was worth the effort to speak, but Ruby answered. 'How old are you, Marian?'

'Fifteen. I'm going to be sixteen next month.'

'Sixteen! My God, when are you going to put some inches on? You look like a midget.'

Marian flushed. She admired Ruby, therefore hated to be criticized by her. 'I don't want to be tall. I like to look up to a guy. It makes me feel so protected.'

'Being that short would make me feel like a freak.'

Marian adroitly changed the subject. 'Norman has an older brother. He's just wild about you, Ruby.'

'Really?' Ruby assumed indifference.

'Yes, he's too much. He's way handsomer than Norman. Girl, if I was only a little older . . .'

'How old is he?'

'Twenty. And that's not all. Their folks have pl – en – ty money. Norman says they're planning on moving up-state somewhere.'

'What did you say his name was?'

'I didn't. But anyhow, it's Orlando. He really flips out over you. He says everytime he sees you he can't eat or sleep. He dreams about you.'

138

'Is that all he says?' The indifferent pose wasn't working, and knowing that I was looking at it slip, she suggested to Marian, 'Look, let's go in the living room and let Phyllisia get some rest.' The relief over being rid of them only lasted a second. The moment silence settled around me, my tension grew. I felt the sheet covering me being tugged, the bed pushed down at my side, as though from the pressure of someone sitting next to me, and as though I had no will of my own, my hand left the protection of the covers and I found myself studying its structure against the light of the lamp on the side of the bed. Of all habits that I had ever acquired in my life, this frightened me most.

'Ruby!' I wanted them around me again with all of their talk, and noise and foolishness, 'Ruby!' My voice was too weak to carry. Pulling back the covers, I swung my feet to the floor, and fighting the darkness brought by the rush of blood to my head, struggled out into the hallway.

Giggles, low and intimate, floated to me from the living room. I tried to hold on to the sounds as a lifeline guiding me. No use. A roaring filled my head that absorbed all sounds. I placed my feet carefully down but it kept on going, going, then, unable to catch myself, I was falling through space. I shouted, 'Ruby, Ruby . . .'

The next I knew, Calvin was standing over me, Ruby by his side. He was shouting and she was crying – hysterically. They were having a terrible quarrel. I was in bed. 'Call the doctor, Daddy. You have to call the doctor,' Ruby cried and Calvin shouted back.

'Don't talk damn foolishness to me, you hear? Ain't the doctor say what's wrong with she? Grief, he say.

What in blazes is that? Ain't we all grieving? It ain't nothing but damn stupidness.'

He stomped out of the room and down the hall to the kitchen. Ruby followed still crying, 'Don't say that. My sister fainted. My sister never fainted in her life. Do you want her to die?'

'Everybody who's going to die around this house, dead. Nobody else dying around here.' Even in my half-conscious state I was impressed. So, he made life and death decisions in this house! 'Nobody, you hear me?' After a short silence he asked, 'What's that?'

'That's her dinner. She can't eat.'

'Oho, is so me money waste on food? Big food to throw to the fish. And she lying looking dead, talking she can't eat. We'll see about this business – can't eat.'

His footsteps, like mortars, pounded the hall and there he was, over me again, pulling the covers from the bed. Ruby pushed herself between us. 'What are you doing to my sister? Leave her alone. I can take care of her.'

Surprised, Calvin stared at Ruby, pulled the skin down beneath her eyes, gazed into them. He felt her head to see if she too might be ill and talking in fever. Satisfied that she was simply out of her mind, he gave her one push that sent her tumbling out of his way.

Then, picking me up from the bed, he carried me down the hall into the kitchen, put me on a chair, pushed it up to the table, placed the tray of food in front of me, unbuckled his belt, and said, 'Now eat!'

I had no choice. I picked up the fork. Too heavy, my hands too weak, it clattered to the table. Ruby rushed to pick it up. Taking some food from the plate she tried to feed me. The belt came down across her back.

'No!' I felt the pain. 'No.'

140

'Pick up that fork,' Calvin commanded. 'And if you drop it one more time, it will be you and me.' Ruby trembled at my side and I knew she was waiting to defend me. To protect her I closed my hand, desperately, around the heavy fork and held on to it.

'Now take some food and put in your mouth,' he ordered. I pushed the fork into the potatoes, managed to get it into my mouth. My body heaved. 'Spit it up,' he challenged. 'Just you spit it up.' At my side Ruby tensed. Calvin wound the belt tighter around his fist. I held the food in my mouth. 'O.K., now swallow.' The potatoes became liquid. I swallowed hard. 'Now get some more.'

He stood there, belt in hand, until I had finished half of the potatoes. He made me drink more milk. Then picked me up, brought me into the living room and put me down on the couch. 'You mother used to say this is the room for the living and this is where I want to see you whenever I come into this house. Unless it's bed-time.' Pointing his finger into Ruby's face he said, 'From now on, if anybody is going to play house around here, is me! I'm going to do the babying and feeding around here. Nobody else!'

The moment he left I heaved. In the bathroom, my face over the toilet bowl, I vomited. I brought up all I had eaten, all I had drunk, and still kept vomiting. Weaker still from my expended energy, I lay on the bathroom floor and cried, 'Mother, why did you leave us alone in this New York with this God-forsaken, cruel brute of a man? How could you do this to us?' At the sound of my words I cried even harder. I cried late into the night. It was the first time I had cried since Mother died.

Ruby resentfully called Calvin's method to make me eat 'operation foodstrap'. But it worked. Every day at an unspecified hour Calvin would burst into the house as though consumed by a great rage. 'Where she?' he would shout. Then, strap in hand, he placed food before me and waited until I had eaten, then went out again. After my night of tears I did not throw up again.

But I hated him! Hatred burned away every other emotion including fear of the spirits haunting me. And I wondered, if there was a spirit in the house, why didn't it haunt Calvin, destroy him or make him destroy himself, instead of bothering me. But nothing happened to him except that he appeared to be more satisfied – like a cat that had stolen milk – with his method. So much so that I was sure I saw him smirking each time he left.

We grew tired of his gloating, Ruby and I. So tired that we decided to trick him. One Saturday Ruby prepared an early lunch, and we had eaten long before he came in shouting, 'Where she?' We both answered at the same time.

'We ate already.'

But he didn't trust us. He looked in the icebox to see what food was missing, searched the garbage pail for the remains. Then, satisfied that we were telling the truth, he said, 'Oho.' Putting his belt back on, he went out, leaving us smug and self-satisfied because for once we had been able to trick him and wipe that stupid smirk off his face.

My strength came back quickly after I had begun to eat. By the end of the second week I was well enough to go back to school.

17

My one desire during my illness was to see Edith. But when I got well, I did *not* go to see her.

I was afraid. If my hatred for Calvin had grown during my convalescence, my fear of him had tripled. I kept out of his way – leaving the house for school before he awoke mornings, securing myself with my studies behind doors evenings when he checked in on us – but his every wish, even his unspoken ones, were law. I came right home from school, made sure to be home early if we went out evenings. And I lacked the courage to visit Edith.

My constant friend was Marian. She lived near, and Calvin appeared to like her. But I found her totally uninteresting, chatty, catty – more Ruby's type – but it was just easier to be friends with *her*.

Before my illness I had already been more serious than Ruby or Marian. After my illness I was even more so. The world had many problems that caught my attention, never theirs. My own problems *also* escaped their notice. One of them was that I had to cram to catch up with my school work. So they annoyed me continually by their frivolity. One afternoon when I was in the middle of study, Marian called and insisted:

'Phyllisia, you must come over right away to see the dress my mother bought.' She was having a party later in the evening to which Ruby and I had been invited.

'No, I can't come now,' I answered. 'Ruby and I will be over later.'

'But you must see it now, Phyllisia. It is *the* gonest...'

'I'm sorry. I have to finish my homework.'

'Oh come on, you don't have to stay but a minute. And besides you have the whole weekend to do your homework.'

'It will just have to wait until later, Marian.' I thought of calling Ruby to take the phone, but changed my mind when I thought of their insipid girl talk. And I would have to be on this end listening.

'Well, look out of the window then. I'll hold it out.'

'Don't be a jackass. I must stick my head out in the cold to see a dress that I'll see later?'

'Oh Phyllisia, don't be that way.'

'Later.' I slammed the phone down and looked at Ruby who sat reading – or pretended to be – on the couch. 'That girl gives me a pain. Clothes and boys, boys and clothes, that's all she ever thinks about.'

Ruby, obviously disappointed that I had not called her to the telephone, said peevishly, 'What's wrong with that? Anyway, you shouldn't talk to her like that. She's your best friend.'

'She gets on my nerves. And as for that mother of hers, she's just as bad. You'd think that all she has to do in this world is to look after Marian's clothes and her boy friends. "Look what I got for Marian,"' I mimicked, 'and, "Norman did this for Marian and Norman did that for Marian." With a mentality like that, what do you expect of the daughter!'

'You're just jealous,' Ruby said maliciously, her head

still bowed to her magazine. 'You know Mrs Robbins isn't that bad.'

'Jealous? Who? Me? You think I'm jealous of Norman? Just because he used to like me? Oh no. Of course it was a low trick for a so-called friend to pull. Going behind my back when I'm sick. But I don't like boys anyhow.'

'They call that sour grapes in this country.'

'Chu–ups,' I sucked my back teeth. 'Just because *all you* think about is boys, that doesn't mean that I do.'

'Then why do you always go over there when Norman is there?'

My mouth fell open. It was she who always insisted that I go. 'Well,' I gasped. 'If that's what you think, then I will stay home and finish my book this evening.'

'You can't do that.' Ruby's attitude underwent a complete change. 'You know I have a date with Orlando.'

'That's you, not me. I have a date to finish my lessons and to read *Native Son*. And *that's* more important to me than listening to you and Marian bleat about the boys.'

'You know that Daddy doesn't want us to go out alone. What if he catches me?'

'That's your headache,' I answered.

'Phyllisia, you can't do that to me. He will skin me alive.' Ruby, who had never done anything wrong, to my knowledge, had *also* developed a fear of Calvin since operation foodstrap.

'All you have to do, Ruby, is tell him that you are seventeen going on eighteen, and that you should be able to cross the street without getting hit by a car, raped or molested.'

'Why don't *you* tell him?'

'Why me? I'm not almost eighteen and I don't want to go out. I want to stay home and study.'

'But I must see Orlando, Phyllisia,' Ruby wailed. 'You know how I feel about him!'

'So you feel so much about him and I must go and listen to all of that garbage you and Marian talk? Then have to hear people say I'm jealous in the bargain?'

'You know I didn't mean it.'

'You never mean anything!' That was exactly the way I felt about them all. They never thought deeply about anything, therefore they were boring, therefore they never 'meant anything.' They took up all of my time, took me away from my work, my thoughts, and they never meant anything.

'If I don't see Orlando, I'll just die.'

'What colour dress do you want to be buried in?'

'Oh Phyllisia!'

'The trouble with you is that you just don't have any courage. If I was almost eighteen and I wanted to see a boy, I would just politely pick up myself and go.'

'You are going on sixteen and I don't see you picking yourself up to go anywhere. Don't tell me that there is no one place that you want to go?'

That hit and hurt. No, I didn't have courage. I wanted to see Edith so badly, and I didn't have the courage to even walk those few blocks to her house, though I knew that I could get there and back without Calvin ever knowing. Still, I answered without blinking, 'No, there is not. And anyhow, there is a lot of difference between fifteen going on sixteen and seventeen going on eighteen.'

'You see how you are?' Ruby's eyes filled with tears. 'I do everything that you want. But when I ask you to do something . . .'

'Don't start that again. After you tell me that I'm jealous and sour grapes and all things like that, don't think I'm going to change my mind just because you cry.'

But I did change my mind. That was another after-effect of my illness. I could not bear to see Ruby cry.

Norman and Orlando were already at Marian's when we arrived. So were two other couples, neither of whom I liked. Marian called them the 'in' group. They were all professional people's children. Ruby and I were allowed in, I was sure, because of Calvin's restaurant, and of course because Ruby was just the coolest chick around.

The entire group spent much time talking about how they couldn't stand Harlem. Norman's and Orlando's father was a doctor. He was moving upstate, but intended keeping his practice in Harlem. The others kept repeating, 'What a fantastic idea,' until Mrs Robbins chimed in, to her credit, 'Yes, it is a great idea. Mr Robbins and I would have moved long ago if we could have *afforded* to.'

Mrs Robbins was sweet and charming. She compensated for having only one child by pretending she was the mother of us all – or, more likely, our sister. She acted as young as the rest of us. Yet she annoyed me – particularly when Norman was around. She looked at me as though she expected me to reach out and grab him.

I sat showing my boredom by looking with disgust at the way Ruby and Marian acted around boys. Marian rolled her eyes and tried to shake her shapeless hips, while Ruby actually became shy and breathless, as weak as though a hard breath would knock her over.

I had been sitting in my corner for a few minutes when Norman asked me to dance. He always asked me to dance, and I usually refused. I was about to say 'no' again when I looked up to see Mrs Robbins level a special-interest stare at us, so I got up. The moment we circled the floor, Norman's arms tightened around me. He put his cheek against mine and whispered in my ear: 'You sure are looking go-od, baby.' I stiffened in disgust at his duplicity, yet felt a certain satisfaction. Marian might have lassoed him but she certainly hadn't tamed him.

'Thank you,' I said harshly.

'Oh don't give that cold-shoulder routine, baby doll. You know I always dug you.'

'You are well taken care of now.'

'I don't know about all of that, baby.'

'Phyllisia.' It was Marian calling from across the room. She either had been keeping her eyes on us or received the high sign from her spy mother. 'Did you see the school pin that Norman gave me?' She stopped dancing to show off the pin she wore on her dress. Norman grinned sheepishly.

Angered by the foolish role that everyone seemed to expect me to play, I said, 'How can you expect me to see *that* across the room as small as it is?'

I refused to dance with Norman again and, sitting in the corner near the hi-fi, began to go through the

148

records. Mrs Robbins came to sit next to me. 'Marian says that the sister of the boy who was killed went to your school,' she said conversationally.

'Sister of what boy? Who was killed?'

'Didn't you hear about it? It was in last week's paper.'

'No, I didn't hear.'

'Now, what was that child's name? I can't remember. Marian, what did you say the name of that child is. The one whose brother was killed?'

'Edith. Edith Jackson. Her brother Randy was killed. You remember her, Phyllisia. She was that sloppy girl who was in your class last year.'

'Yes, Jackson. That's the name,' Mrs Robbins agreed. 'A policeman shot him. Said that he was running across a parking lot and told him to halt. Shot once in the air, he said, but the boy never stopped running. Shot him in the back. They say the boy died instantly.'

Randy dead? I would never see him again? I thought of him as I had last seen him, resentful, angry. I had never liked him much – but not to see him again! It was impossible!

'Is that the Edith who came up to our house?' Ruby asked. 'I know her. She was a good friend of Phyllisia's.'

'For God's sake, no!' Marian exclaimed, horrified. 'That beat-up looking chick?'

'Marian, nobody can look *that* bad,' Norman laughed.

'Worse than that,' Marian cried. 'She looks like the last thing that the dogs dragged in.'

'I think she's a nice-looking girl,' Ruby defended her mildly. 'She just needs a little fixing up, that's all.'

'You must be kidding,' Marian laughed. 'It would take more than a Christian miracle to do anything for *that* chick.'

I hated her! I hated them all! Every laughing, belly-to-belly-dancing one of them! But Marian worst of all! Talking about *my* friend – my best friend! Why, Edith was a hundred times better and more decent than any single one of them! Even Ruby did not have the decency to stop dancing when she talked of Randy's death! I would never *forgive her* for that either. And I would never again call Marian 'friend'.

Without a word I got up and went into the bedroom to search for my coat. Mrs Robbins' voice kept up, 'My husband is so upset about the shooting. He says this police brutality has got to stop. He says that there are just too many black boys who get shot just because they run.'

And Marian's voice, flat, inexpressive, 'But Ma. People are supposed to stop running if a policeman orders them to. They know that if they don't they will be shot.'

Norman answered, 'I don't know about that. If a policeman had a gun and was shooting, I'd be too scared to stop.'

'Yeah,' Orlando's heavy voice agreed. 'Different people react in different ways. No telling what folks are likely to do.' The music stopped and started again. The shuffling feet of the dancers never stopped.

18

It took me only ten minutes to cover the distance from Marian's to Edith's house, but when I arrived, I didn't go in. I could not. I stood looking into the darkened hallway of the building up the rickety, wooden steps, telling myself that Edith needed me. That she had come to me when Mother died. That I should go to her now. I told myself that she was alone, more so with her burdens than I had ever been, and that she needed a friend more than ever. But I did not go in.

Instead my fears worked on me. What if I went into that hallway and someone seized me, attacked me, raped me? What if someone caught me and injected dope in my arm and ruined me forever? I had heard about that happening.

And Randy was a thief! I knew it. Suppose he had stolen things and had hidden them in the house? Suppose the police were there, searching the house and found them, just as I walked in? They would arrest me! They would call Calvin . . . Sad, bewildered, guilty, I walked away from the stoop. Perhaps, after all, the old friendship was better off finished.

When I returned, the party was over. Mrs Robbins met me at the door. 'Where in the world did you go, child? Your sister was looking all over for you. I told her that you must have gone home.'

'Where is she now?'

'She just left. Marian and the boys walked home with her.'

I met Marian and the boys on the way. They were talking all at once. Then I noticed that Orlando was being supported on either side by Marian and Norman and that he was holding a bloody handkerchief to his nose. My heart jumped.

'What's happened? Where's Ruby?' For answer Marian flipped her fingers, indicating trouble. I flew to the house.

Long before I reached the door, I heard Ruby's shrieks. 'I didn't do anything, I didn't do anything, Daddy.' Her cries were deafening. Calvin was beating her! And he had hit Orlando!

Now he was shouting: 'You will shame me? You think you will bring shame down on me head?' With each word I heard the crack of the strap and Ruby's scream. Without thinking I rushed into the apartment, into the living room and threw myself at Calvin. For a frantic moment I felt his terrible strength as we grappled for the belt, then I found myself on the floor scrambling to my feet. 'All you think I'm a fool . . .' The belt descended as I leaped. I held it in my hand and Calvin swung me like a pendulum. I held tight. The action calmed him, relieved him of his anger, although his thinned lips were still ringed with ash, his eyes still bulged like those of a madman.

'All you think that you will run me crazy, huh? I'll take your tails and ship it right back to The Island. I tell all you to go together and come back together. But no, you want to fool me.'

152

Looking accusingly at me, he pointed. 'You let she go ahead so she can take care of she dirty business. Then you come behind and expect me to think that all you together all the time. You can't spit in me eye and tell me it's raining outside. I ain't recent born!'

It was slow dawning, but suddenly it was clear. Calvin's anger had nothing to do with my leaving the party. He was really angry at *Ruby*. Now I felt free to defend both of us. 'We did go together. And we didn't do anything wrong.'

'How you talking?' His eyes blazed at me. 'And I ain't see this one here downstairs in this very house ready to do rudeness?'

'I did not,' Ruby cried. 'I never . . .'

'Because I catch your tail good,' he shouted. 'If I ain't come just then, so help me God, I know what would happen!'

Stunned was too mild a word for how I felt, but I never shifted my eyes from Calvin. 'Not again,' he shouted. 'Never again! You will keep all you backsides where it belong from now on. Right in this house!'

I never looked at Ruby while Calvin was in the room, but when he went out I turned on her: 'Ruby, you didn't . . .'

'I didn't do anything,' she sobbed.

'But Daddy says he saw you start . . .'

'No such a thing. Marian an – and Norman an – and Orlando walked me home. An – and Orlando walked me to the foot of the stair and asked me to kiss him goo – good-night.'

I couldn't be hearing right. 'Ruby, you mean you let Orlando kiss you downstairs in *this* house?'

153

'Ye – yes.'

'Ruby, you didn't!'

Was she mad! How could she do a thing like that within a one-mile radius of where Calvin *might* be. Then it came to me: Ruby had never had *reason* to fear Calvin as I had, therefore she had never been as secretive as I. But I said in disgust, 'My God, Ruby, how could you ever do anything so stupid!'

Later in bed she said to me, 'You know, Phyllisia. We have to go to Daddy and explain that it's not the way he thinks at all.'

'Explain to him!' Now I knew she *was* out of her mind! The welts of his belt were still on her back and here she was talking as though she had already forgotten the beating. 'Look, Ruby, Daddy doesn't care what you have to say. If he did, he would have listened to you in the first place.'

'But, Phyllisia, didn't you hear him say that he would keep us in the house – that we can't go out any more?'

'I can suffer all the tortures that Calvin Cathy can give,' I said proudly, 'but I will never go to him and beg. Never in my life!'

19

I *did* suffer tortures. But it was because I had not gone to Edith. And I could not go now.

I blamed my not going to my friend on Calvin. I blamed it on him, strangely enough, because he was wrong about Ruby. True, I had never really liked him. He was mean, he shouted too much, and he gave stupid orders for us to obey. But beneath my dislike I had always been convinced that he was right. Now he had been wrong about Ruby and I asked myself, had he ever been right about anything?

Right or wrong, he had the advantage of being our father, and we were his prisoners. After the night of the party he ordered us to be in the house at all times, after school. On weekends, if he permitted us to go to the movies, he checked up on us even then. We saw him near the theatre spying on our movements. The only things we were given permission to do were our homework, the housework, looking at TV and looking out of the window – at other people having fun. At least that's what we were *supposed* to do.

Ruby did. She obeyed all orders. Rushing home from school, she cooked, cleaned, did her homework and looked out of the window. I refused. How could someone who had never been right about anything have such complete control over people's lives? Over my life?

Whenever I thought about it, my resentment grew. I refused to be his prisoner. I did not hurry home from school. I stopped doing homework, did no housework. I came home when I pleased, yet it was usually earlier than I wanted because of Ruby. She was lonely and unhappy. She would meet me at the door crying, 'Where did you go?'

'Walking.'

'How can you go walking and leave me here all by myself?' I hated to hurt her, but she seemed to like being hurt. 'Why don't *you* go walking sometimes? Why do you come rushing home and expect me to be with you?'

I didn't really do anything. I walked alone. I had no best friend. Even if I had wanted to be friendly with Marian, which I didn't, I couldn't. Calvin had accused Mr and Mrs Robbins of running a house for fast girls. Now Marian and I were forbidden to see each other. I did not want any other friends. I liked being alone; besides, Ruby was enough for me.

'It's a good thing that I did come home. Daddy was here and he asked for you.' I shrugged. 'I told him that you went to the library.' I shrugged again. Shrugging had become my permanent answer, and the library had become my permanent excuse.

When Calvin caught me out of the house he would ask, 'Where you been?' I would say, 'The library.' 'What library? I was waiting for you to come out and I ain't see you. They only have one door to that library.' And I would ask what library. 'What library but the one on 136th Street!' Then I would explain, 'But Daddy, I went to the 42nd Street library. That's the only one that has the books I need.' He would stare at me not knowing what to believe and I would stare back thinking, you are the one who is never wrong. Prove that I'm lying.

'Phyllisia, what's happening to you?' Ruby complained. 'You are changing so much.' I shrugged. I was changing. I felt the change big in me. I now hated school, hated people – everybody, except Ruby. My thoughts were disordered. I no longer read, hardly even thought any more.

'Daddy made me give him your report card. He was so upset when he saw it he said he was going to your school one day this week.'

A familiar fear raced through me but I closed it out. He would find out that I had been signing my own report card. I shrugged. 'Let him come. What does he think? That he can beat sense in my head?' He couldn't, but I knew he would try. I was waiting.

'There's Orlando,' Ruby said wistfully, from her favourite spot at the window. 'Just think he used to like me so much, now he doesn't even look up here.'

'Scared to death,' I said sarcastically. This brought a fresh flow of tears from Ruby.

'This isn't living. This is merely existing,' she said, throwing back her head. Ruby had seen some movie actress or the other go through the appropriate dramatic scene, and this pathetic imitation was all she could come up with in her inner struggle against Calvin! No, Calvin had no worry at all with Ruby. His biggest worry was me. He knew it and I knew it.

And so it was not too great a surprise to me when Mr Charles and Cousin Frank paid us an 'unexpected' visit one day when Ruby and I were alone. For her it was a treat from the gods – the first company we had since my illness, and the first male voices besides Calvin's that we had heard in the apartment. They came in with outstretched arms, and Ruby rushed to embrace them and be embraced by them. I didn't. I had loved them once, but this time when they came, after their long absence, I suspected they were here to spy for Calvin.

'Eheh,' Cousin Frank regarded me, his cigar hanging in surprise from the corner of his mouth. 'But this one get too grown to kiss?'

'That's what we get for staying away so long.' Mr Charles smiled his soft, relaxed smile. 'I'm happy to see they even remember me.'

'But,' Cousin Frank said, 'I'm a Cathy and so I expect a big rush and kiss and squeeze the minute I get in the door. However, here we are.'

They made themselves comfortable. To my suspicious eyes, they were a little too relaxed, too comfortable. And I was right. No sooner did they appear to be at their ease than Cousin Frank said to me, somewhat jokingly: 'Your father tells me he's having a little trouble with you.'

'What trouble?' I asked. 'No trouble. We are here, his prisoners, and cannot leave the house. What trouble is that?'

'Eheh, but listen to this girl talk, Charles.' He had a habit of looking astonished with a twinkle in his eyes. 'She talking grown.'

'She look grown,' Mr Charles countered. 'She bigger than you now, ain't it?' He spoke to Ruby.

It was true. Since my illness I had developed rapidly. My breasts were fuller than Ruby's now, so were my legs and thighs. I had even grown an inch or two taller than she.

'Yes,' Ruby answered, anxious to talk. 'She got big so fast that when I asked Daddy for money to buy her new clothes, he asked me where she had been and what she was doing – meaning rudeness – you know?'

The two men exchanged glances and Cousin Frank cried: 'What! What kind of nonsense is this?'

Encouraged now, Ruby rushed on. 'Yes, it's like Phyllisia says, he keeps us prisoners in here and blames it all on a party we went to . . .' She never stopped talking and the men listened gravely. Then Mr Charles' massive face began to crumble into its jigsaw puzzle look: 'But the man must be sick. How does he think that he can get away with these things in this year of our Lord and the Blessed Virgin Mary too?

'But what get me, it's we he call to say that *he's* having troubles. But from the look of it, it's that you children are the ones with troubles.'

Looking at me he asked, 'What's this I hear about school?' I shrugged. Not sharing Ruby's confidence in Calvin's friends, I saw no reason why I should discuss my affairs with them. 'As I recall,' he went on, 'you used to be the smart one in the family. What happened?' I only shrugged again. 'And you used to like me and trust me,' he added.

Did I? If I did, it was a long time ago. And for some adverse reason I remembered that they had been in the house the day of the riot, when Calvin had first threatened me about Edith, and neither had done anything to defend me.

'But you must be leaving something out,' Mr Charles insisted, concentrating on Ruby. 'You mean to tell me that he *actually* beat *you*, and all you were doing was kissing . . .'

'I swear I'm not leaving anything out, Mr Charles. Orlando asked me if he could kiss me, and I said yes. It all happened so fast. I didn't even have a chance to kiss him good, and Daddy . . .'

'But you must be eighteen?'

'In two months.'

'Did you ever kiss a boy?'

'No. Never.'

'That,' Cousin Frank said, taking his cigar out of his mouth, 'is a sin and a shame.'

Fascinated I kept my gaze on the cigar. It had seemed such an immovable part of his face, and that he had been shocked into taking it out of his mouth made him look a bit strange, and more sincere.

'Frank, you say you are some kind of relative to these children, and you mean to tell me that knowing the Cathys firsthand, and knowing they are a crazy bunch, the lot of them, and Calvin in particular, you ain't give the children one minute of your time since their mother's death?'

Irritated, Cousin Frank snapped, returning his cigar into its corner, 'But what you think I'm doing here? I know Calvin ain't got the mind to take care of children. Even if his heart got good intentions, his mind is too busy and his ways are too mad.'

'The question is,' Charles said, 'what is to be done under these conditions.'

'What would you suggest?'

'You said it already, Frank. It's hard to get Calvin to sit still to listen to reason – number one. And number two – he's busy, busy all the time. Best thing is that they go back home.'

Back to The Island? I hadn't thought about home for

160

a long time. What would it be like to live among plants and trees, near the sea again? I liked the idea. Yet I felt hardened – a part of the concrete buildings and side-walks of the city.

'We could talk to him about it, of course,' Cousin Frank said dubiously. 'But I wonder if he might not object. After all, they are little bits of his flesh and blood – all that he have. He might not want the separa-tion.' What an idea! The way Calvin hated us!

But surprisingly, Mr Charles agreed. 'True. The only other thing I see – Frank, you are not married. Why don't you move in here to keep an eye on things?'

'What!'

'After all, he is *your* cousin.'

'Me! Live under the same roof with Calvin? I love these children, it's true. I also love my cousin. But you will never get *me* to stay one day in the same house with him. What? With his big talk, his big plans, he's too big-time for me. We'll drive each other mad! Better that they come stay with me.'

'But you don't have space.'

'I'll find space – ain't you got that big house?'

'No vacancies.'

'Anyhow, wait, let's talk to Calvin. See what he have in mind.' Cousin Frank reached for the telephone.

'What are you doing?' Ruby cried in terror. 'Are you telling him what I said?'

I gave her an I-told-you-so look. Stupid ass! Dribbling like a brook from her mouth!

'Look, your father is no monster,' Cousin Frank re-buked her sternly. 'He might not always agree, but you can always talk to him.' And he picked up the phone.

Calvin breezed into the house a short time later with

the loud laughter and hearty greetings that he reserved for friends. 'Eheh, but I ask you to come and see the children, not call a convention. Taking me away from business. Ain't got much help, you know. Anyway, I come.'

'But did you drive or did you fly? You got here quicker than it take to say Willie Mays,' Mr Charles laughed, and Cousin Frank teased:

'He think that maybe somebody is making off with one of his girls. And it's true, you know. Pretty, pretty people so. Some tin-can soldier in a helicopter will swoop down from the sky one day and – pufft – gone.' Calvin's eyebrows quivered at the joke.

Ruby huddled in a corner of the couch, and I sat next to her – a buffer between her and Calvin, in case he got mad when he heard how much she had been blabbing.

'But Frank, how come I ain't see you?' he said to his cousin. 'I must call you to come and look in on your *own* family?'

'They say a bad excuse is better than none. But I ain't giving none. I guilty as hell.'

'I think you spit me out because me wife dead.'

'Give me a better reason to spit you out?'

They joked and laughed, old-talked, and never once mentioned the reason why they had all gathered here. Calvin brought out a well-hidden bottle of rum, and they drank and relaxed and talked and joked. It seemed they were only there to pass the time. After a while Mr Charles became serious.

'I hate to break up a fete, Calvin. But it is important business that we are here to talk about this evening.' He sounded like a preacher; they all fell into a church mood, and it became clear that, after all, they had been merely letting the minutes pass, waiting to choose the right one. 'I know too that it's a long time since I come here. What excuse.' Mr Charles opened his hands in a futile gesture. 'The same thing. Always the same thing. I busy. We bust out our brains trying to make money and we let the essential things get scrambled in the process. But the strange thing, Calvin, even before you call, I had made up me mind to come.

'For the last three nights I dream of Ramona. She come to me plain, plain like anything. Just like if I awake. "Charles," she say to me, "The children, Charles, go see about the children."'

'Now you know that I ain't one for jombies and things. Perhaps it was just me bad conscience. But the minute you call, I drop everything and come. And I say, is lucky.'

Calvin leaned back in his chair, listening, his hands shielding his eyes. And Mr Charles went on. 'The things that I hear from Ruby here, make me scalp crawl like it got worms in it.'

'And what did you hear from the *little* one? That she live in the library?' Calvin quipped sardonically.

Showing his annoyance, Cousin Frank retorted, 'Don't tell me they can't go to the library. My God, Calvin, you are really mad.'

'You ain't know what you talking,' Calvin answered. 'Every time you hear, is library, library, library, and every time she go she school marks shoot down to zed.' The shield of his hands dropped from his eyes and he stared at me. I stared back. I did not reply, I only looked and thought hard enough for him to read in my eyes: Prove that I don't! 'See how rude she is.' Calvin pointed threateningly at me.

The truce was over. Ruby sank further into the corner. But Mr Charles took up our defence, calmly. 'We understand that you are making prisoners of these girls.' After a short silence, 'But how, Calvin?'

'Yes, how?' Cousin Frank blazed, angered by Calvin's silence. 'How you mean, how? The man mad, I tell you. He a fool!' He was, after all very much like Calvin.

'Come, come,' Mr Charles soothed. 'We'll get nowhere with a row.'

'But he must know!' Cousin Frank charged. 'We have a responsibility!'

'Yes, yes,' Mr Charles said. 'But let Calvin explain, nuh. He must have *his* reasons. After all, we have been away a long time, Frank. And although we are long overdue for this talk, we just can't barge in here and take over.'

'O.K.' Cousin Frank agreed, trying to regain his calm. 'O.K., tell your reason, Calvin. Because we want you to know that we can't afford to let these conditions go on.'

Calvin smiled and shook his head in disbelief. 'But it's *me* who ask *you* to come here to talk to the little one. And here it's *me* you bawling out. Frank, why?'

'Tell me what you expected Phyllisia to do under these conditions, Calvin?' Charles stayed calm, remained the controlling figure in the discussion. 'After all, she was always a little strong-willed. Did you expect her to submit to being a prisoner?'

'But what does he intend to do about it?' Cousin Frank was close to losing his temper again.

164

Calvin did not answer immediately. He sat looking perfectly relaxed in his chair, a big hulk of man, staring at the floor, absorbing every word that was said. Yet when he looked up he said simply, 'What to do?' Flinging his arms out in a gesture of helplessness he repeated, 'What to do?

'You say *you* busy. What about me? But I must look after them. I must see that they eat, sleep and go to school and that no mischief come to them. How can I do that when I'm working every day and they gallivanting all over New York?'

'We know that it's not easy, Calvin,' Mr Charles agreed. 'And we know we have not helped. I think that I can talk for Frank as well as myself when I say that we will take more interest. We will be here much more often. But even with that, Calvin, you have to be able to trust your children.'

'That's the trouble,' Calvin protested. 'How you can trust two girls, big so? The other day I come home and guess what?'

'Please, Calvin,' Cousin Frank waved his hand in utter disgust. 'Don't tell me about seeing the older one kissing a boy good-night.'

'Exactly!'

'What you want her to kiss? A girl?'

Mr Charles held his hand up for peace. 'But Calvin,' he said quietly, 'Ruby is almost eighteen!'

'That's when things does happen.'

'At her age it can happen anytime. You can't be on top of her all the time. You work. She goes to school. Even if her mother was alive, she would do what she wanted. You must have faith in her.'

'It ain't she,' Calvin replied evasively. 'It's the

boys I don't trust. You must remember when we were boys . . .'

'Don't say we!' Cousin Frank exploded. 'Say you! Never in all my days before or since, have I seen a male, be he dog, cat or man, so bold as you. Don't take that out on these children. True, the Bible say that the sins of the parents and all like that – but it ain't mean it that way.'

'Be that as it may,' Mr Charles' soft voice intervened again. 'You know you don't make sense, Calvin. Because you don't trust the boys you lock up the girls?'

'Lock up? They go out, to school, the movies. They got keys . . .'

'Calvin! Even you must know that children need more than school or an occasional movie. They must have a broader life.'

'Yes, yes, I intend that they should have it. The minute I see my way clear, I'll be taking them around, I'll see to it.'

'You!' Cousin Frank was in a rage. 'They must wait around for *you*? Ain't I tell you, Charles, the man mad! The best thing for me to do is pick them up right now and take them over to my place.'

'Now, now, Frank,' Mr Charles tried to calm him. 'There is nothing wrong with a parent taking out his children. As a matter of fact, it's a good thing. But what to do in the meantime, Calvin? Must they wait until you settle all your business?'

Calvin placed his hands flatly down on the arms of the chair. 'I hear everything that you are saying. I'm listening. But I cannot let them go out in the streets unprotected. I – I – I trust them. But you must remember they

166

are not American girls. They don't know nothing about New York.'

'Have you thought about sending them back home? I mean until you find the time or until you feel they are old enough . . .'

'No!' Calvin's no was emphatic. 'No, man, I'm not going to burden me sister with me problems!'

'Then they must come with me!' Cousin Frank's voice was equally as emphatic.

'No!' Calvin said again. 'Ramona wanted them here and here is where they stay!

'And besides . . .' His face began to quiver and quiver, his eyebrows, the muscles of his cheek began jerking and twitching. He was going to make a most difficult confession. 'And besides I – I – I *want* them here with me!'

20

So, he wanted us with him!

He should never have let me know. Like a camel sensing water in a desert, I sensed a spot somewhere in him that I could touch and hurt. I intended to go after it.

But his words had a different effect on Ruby. 'Poor Daddy,' she said when we were going to bed. 'I really believe that he likes us but doesn't know how to show it.' While the men had been talking, I had been studying her, watching as her expression changed from one of self-pity to compassion. So I was ready.

'Believe it if it makes you happy,' I said tartly.

'We should really go to him, show him that we will be good and . . .'

'And what *have* you been showing him, sitting in the house pining and crying and acting the jackass?'

'We can at least talk to him, Phyllisia.' She returned my long, hard look with a plea. 'After all, he really isn't a monster.'

'You talk to him,' I shrugged. 'But don't you expect me to hang on to any more straps keeping it off your backsides.' Deliberately I turned my back to her and fell asleep formulating my plan.

It was spring. A lovely spring. The clear blue of the sky, catching the warm brilliance of the sun, kept scattering it generously about so that it touched even the grimy corners of the city. It was exactly the kind of weather designed for doing things – exciting things, especially the kind of death-defying things one plans and puts into action.

That morning I took longer to get out of bed and delayed so long with my toilet and dressing that Ruby was forced to leave the house before me. Then around the time that Norman usually left for school, I went out. He was already near the corner when I left the house, and I had to run to catch up. 'Hey, Norman.' I slowed down as I neared him, wanting to see his expression as he turned and recognized me. One could call it instant fright when he first looked, then it calmed down to tension and discomfort.

'Oh – oh, hi, Phyllisia.'

'It's a lovely day, isn't it?' I prayed that my smile was provocative.

'Uhhuh.'

'It's such a lovely day that I think I'll go to the park and just lie around on the grass instead of going to school.'

'Uhuh.'

'Do *you* have to go to school?'

'Who me . . .? Look, Phyllisia, the park is a great idea but I would not like to go with you. Your old man is too much of a blow-top. You chicks are just too dangerous even to be seen with.' With that he quickened his steps, leaving me far behind.

My embarrassment over the snub heightened my anger against Calvin, my determination to make him pay. I did not go to school that day and for most of that week. I went to the movies, discovered and explored

169

midtown Manhattan, went into restaurants to eat lunch, and I went to the park.

I met José in the park. José was a handsome Puerto Rican boy. I was lying on the grass beneath a tree – just lying there, looking up at the branches, when I heard this voice and looked around, and I saw him standing there looking at me. 'Oh *bonita, bonita.*' His accent as well as his admiration was exaggerated but that did not stop me from liking it. 'You're the girl I have been looking for all of my life,' he said. This approach was something I had read about, never expected to hear. It gave me a thrill of excitement, of danger. Yet I didn't fall for him right off. He just seemed the perfect answer to get even with Calvin.

'I bet you say that to all the girls.' I had not wanted to use that tired old line, but it was all I could think of.

'No, *mi vida.* It is you who are the most beautiful.' I smiled, lowering my eyelashes, as I had seen Ruby do. 'For another girl I have no eyes. And you know, I was just saying to myself, if I see the one of my heart I will take her rowing and sing to her. Do you like to row – in a boat . . .?'

We went rowing. We walked around the park. We ate hot dogs at a pushcart. And José kept saying the nicest foreign things to me. It grew late and it was time to go but I had made up my mind to stay out later than usual. I insisted that we stay longer, and José thought it was because I wanted to make love. He tried to kiss me. I fought him. He thought I was pretending and kept wrestling. Soon we grew tired and ended up sitting on the grass holding hands. We were both bored. I, with fighting. He, with holding hands. But we made a date for the next day.

Ruby was waiting at the door when I came in. 'Phyllisia, where have you been? I thought something had happened to you.'

'Something did, Ruby. I have a boy friend.'

'Boy friend? Where did you meet him?'

'In the park. He is tall, about eighteen . . .'

'In the park! Phyllisia, did you go to school today?'

'No, I haven't been to school for days.'

'Daddy'll kill you!'

'Let him. What did he say today when he came home to check up?'

'He didn't come home. He telephoned. He said to tell you to call him when you came in.'

It was almost eight o'clock. I stared at the telephone, but I didn't move to touch it. It was no good staying out late if he didn't find out about it. *Let* him find out. But I hadn't worked up the nerve to *tell* him. 'Call him,' Ruby insisted. 'Tell him that you came home a long time ago but I forgot to tell you.' I shook my head – no. 'Please, Phyllisia, I think he listened to Mr Charles last week. I think he wants to trust us more.'

'Believe it if it makes you happy,' was my glib retort. I refused to telephone.

Then next morning, when he heard us moving around, he got up and came into our room. 'What happened to you,' he said. 'Didn't I tell you to call me when you came home?'

'I forgot to tell her,' Ruby put in before I could answer.

'Forgot to tell her?' He looked from one to the other of us, weighing whether he should believe her. Then he warned, 'Don't forget again, you hear me?'

Ruby and I left the house together to take the subway

downtown. When she got off to change trains, I rode one stop down and doubled back, and rushed to meet José in the park. José took me to the movies that day, and all during the picture I had to keep moving his hand from my leg. Later we went to the park and ate hot dogs. José called me *bonita* and *mi vida*. We walked holding hands, and I went home late again.

'Are you going to call Daddy?' Ruby demanded. I shook my head – no. 'Phyllisia, why are you doing this? Daddy is acting nicer and you are just showing him you can't be trusted. He'll think that he can't trust me too.' I answered with a shrug.

The next day was Saturday. I expected Calvin to come in to us ranting and raving. But he didn't. When he awoke about eleven that morning, we had already had our breakfast and were cleaning the house, preparing to go out to our Saturday movie. He dressed and left the house without speaking to us. That worried me. It worried Ruby too. It seemed to me that he had deliberately created a deep silence in the house. A waiting silence.

The weekend passed without incident, without one word being shouted at us. And on Monday, when we were on our way to the subway, Ruby asked: 'Are you going to see that boy today?'

'Yes.'

'I'm going to call Cousin Frank and Mr Charles and tell.'

'Call them. Who cares?'

'Phyllisia, you don't even know that boy. Suppose he does nastiness to you . . .'

'Then Daddy will send us home quicker.'

'Home? You don't mean that, Phyllisia. You don't want to go back to The Island!'

'Sure I do. It would be better than staying here.'

'But I don't want to go back home!'

'You don't! You mean you'd rather stay here and be a prisoner?'

'But we're not like prisoners any more. I told you Daddy was changing.'

'Ruby, I don't understand you. You really act as though you like that man.'

'Why shouldn't I? After all he *is* my father!' She walked angrily from me, never looking back. I finally closed my mouth when she disappeared from view, and hurried on to the park.

That day we only walked and ate hot dogs. I had to pay because José had run out of money. But even at that, when we were parting that evening, José said to me: 'Look, Phyllisia, you are *bonita* and *mi vida* and all of that, but I'm not coming out every day and missing time from school just to hold hands.'

'What do you think I am?' I demanded in my most offended voice. 'Do you think that I'm one of those girls who you can do what you want with?'

'Christ, no. But at least give me a kiss. Let me know I got something to look forward to. My God, holding hands!'

His decision was in his tone. If I didn't let him kiss me, I would lose him as a companion. I needed some-one to walk around the park with. So I decided to let him kiss me.

I didn't know it would be like that! He put his arms around me and his mouth – soft, wet over mine. It felt nasty, at first. But then his breath came hot and fast, and he held me tight. His body was hard against mine. How strong he was. Stronger, much stronger than when we had wrestled. I pushed against him but could not get away. When he finally let me go, I ran. I was in love. I heard José laughingly call after me: '*Mañana, mi vida, mañana.*'

Tomorrow it would happen. I knew it! Tomorrow we would meet and kiss and it would happen! Walking home, I didn't even think of Calvin, or of spiting him, or of trying to make him send us back to The Island. I only thought of José, José, José. How exciting it was. How thrilling it was to be in love – and how frightening. My cheeks were hot and my lips were sore and burning from that kiss and I knew that if I looked into a mirror my eyes would be shining, lighting up my secret insides.

21

When I got home, Mr Charles and Cousin Frank were there. They were sitting in the living room with Ruby and they were more serious than I had ever seen them. I knew I was in for a good talk and tried to smother the glow in my eyes. I only succeeded in looking guilty and acting sullen.

'Your father just went out,' Cousin Frank said. I was sure this was a finger of accusation.

'He was so mad,' Ruby was evidently distressed. 'He was mad enough to kill you.'

'Let him kill me. Who cares?' I said shrugging.

'Well, as it happens, we do,' Cousin Frank answered, and Mr Charles backed him up.

'That's right, we do. Pretty girl like you, we wouldn't want *anything* to happen to you.' I didn't look at either of them. I couldn't. But my face burned at the shades of meaning in his voice. 'The other evening, after our talk, I had the distinct feeling that your father would slacken up a bit, grant you more privileges.'

'What privileges,' I snapped, glad to be on the safe ground of condemning Calvin. 'He didn't tell *me* anything about any privileges.'

'No,' Mr Charles spoke softly. 'That is not Calvin's way. But even Ruby tells us that he has been much easier. He hasn't been checking up . . .'

'So what is that? We still can't go anywhere.'

'Haven't *you* been somewhere?' Cousin Frank asked sharply.

'He didn't let me,' I said evasively. 'I just went.'

'But we just can't pick up and go where we want,' Cousin Frank said. 'This is a big city. It can be an ugly city. Even on The Island you couldn't just pick up and go.'

'On The Island I wasn't a prisoner!' I answered rudely, and Mr Charles quickly took over.

'Phyllisia, Phyllisia, we know how badly things have been handled. Calvin is our friend as well as a member of Frank's family. We know he has strange ways of doing things. But give the man a chance. I beg you. Everything that everybody do in this world can be done a different way. Now, take this boy that you have as a friend, why shouldn't you be able to invite him to your home?' I shot a dirty look at Ruby. My God, but that girl had a big mouth. 'Yes, your sister called us to tell us, and with good reason too. If we hadn't come, your father would have still been here waiting for you, and God alone knows what would have happened.'

'The way I see it,' Cousin Frank put in, 'is that things are going too far too fast.'

'We made him leave,' Mr Charles said. 'But I can't see us leaving, knowing he will come in later and . . .'

'These things must be resolved,' Cousin Frank said. 'The sooner the better. Or else tomorrow we might have to piece you together like a jigsaw puzzle.'

'Yes,' Mr Charles agreed, getting to his feet. 'Let us go over to his place and try to make some sense out of this nonsense. Don't you agree, little Phyllisia?' He touched my hair smiling.

176

We went by car, and it seemed that no sooner had we entered the car than it was time to get out again. I had no idea that Calvin's restaurant was so near to home. Yet judging from the frequency that he popped in and out of the house I should have known. Mr Charles parked the car, we were out on the sidewalk being led into the restaurant, and Ruby and I were still looking around for this restaurant that my father owned. When I saw it, I stopped at the door. I did not want to enter.

The opening of the restaurant was a slit in the wall. A small neon sign with the words HOME COOKING in the window distinguished it from the row of buildings and small storefronts crowding the avenue. It was a warm night, but inside the restaurant was hot. Men, rough-looking, with clothes grimy from work, sat along the counter, sweating and gulping down food, some laughing and talking in loud voices, some cursing. Others crowded the narrow aisle behind, waiting to be seated. Behind the counter two harassed men worked. Aprons covered them from their waist down, but on top they wore polo shirts, and sweat from their efforts to keep serving the customers poured down their necks and stuck their shirts to their bodies. They added to the din by shouting orders to a cook in the kitchen behind them. One of the two men was my father.

Shrinking against the wall to stay away from the hot, sweaty bodies, I followed Mr Charles, Cousin Frank and Ruby up the narrow aisle. As I neared the elbow of the counter, my gaze settled, suddenly and terrifyingly, on a man sitting there. He was a small man, wispy, with a battered felt hat pulled down over his forehead. He reminded me of Edith's father. He looked up as I approached and caught my startled stare with faded old eyes.

Then he bowed his head to concentrate on his food and on his shaking hands, which tried to control the fork on its way to his mouth.

We squeezed into the long, narrow kitchen with the cook who was sweating over the steam table as he passed out the orders through the horizontal opening to the men serving the counter. Calvin joined us there.

'So you bring your tail home?' He had eyes only for me. But the two men placed themselves between us, and Mr Charles began. 'Calvin, we come here because you left in such a huff that we know you thinking of something crazy. Now we think we can settle this once and for always.'

'Is settled,' Calvin snapped angrily. 'You see me? I ain't got time for stupidness. But take my word. It's settled.'

'Who know your business better than you,' Cousin Frank ventured. 'But you know as well as we, this business is getting out of hand.'

'There is just too much misunderstanding all around,' Mr Charles' soft voice strained to be heard over the loud customers talking in front. 'If we could only this once . . .'

'Charles, Frank,' Calvin said impatiently. 'I listen good to all you the other day and I tell you me head need examined. Look at what I get for it. I tell you, just look what I get. This one here all footloose and gallivanting? No more! I ain't taking no more . . .'

'Hey, West Indian,' a voice interrupted from the front. 'What the hell all this 'bout? What the hell man here mean he ain't serving me . . .?'

We all looked out at the lisping speaker. A drunk

reeling and rearing off his seat. 'I ain't done 'im nothin'. I ain't done no-body nothin'.' He was so drunk, so dishevelled, dirty, that the work-soiled men at the counter suddenly looked like businessmen by comparison. 'What he mean ain't servin' . . .'

'What happening?' Calvin yelled to the counterman. 'Ain't the man got money?'

'I don't know what he got, Calvin. But he too dru . . .'

'If the man got money, give him food. If he ain't, throw him out!'

Then he turned back to us. 'You see I busy. Too busy to take foolishness. But I'll tell you one thing. You give me some good advice the other night and I'm taking it. I'm taking their backsides and shipping it out of here. Shipping them right back home. But I tell you, God help me that I ain't got to kill this one before she go!'

22

I had forgotten all about Edith.

My efforts to spite Calvin and my 'affair' with José had wiped all thought of her from my mind. But my visit to Calvin's restaurant reopened the spot that she occupied like a festering sore. Memories – or more – the feeling that was Edith – poured back in.

The next day when I awoke I was sick. Sick with a fever that burned thoughts of José to a withering ash, and scorched everything and everyone else into unimportance. Only Edith remained, standing out, indestructible, her big round eyes tormented, accusing. I knew it was because I was going to die. Something inside, something that had been sustaining me, had crumbled, my strength had been destroyed.

In the depth of my misery I heard Ruby cackling over me, mother-hen fashion. I was dimly aware of her when she came to the obvious conclusion that I could not go to school. Later, Calvin pushed open the door of our room and shouted something to me. I did not hear. I suppose I did not want to. How could I stand the burden of another order, another threat, when at any rate I was dying of shame at the thought of 'his restaurant!'

When the door slammed behind him, I drew my knees up to touch my forehead, rolled myself up under the bedcovers to emphasize my aloneness in the apartment – to keep out all light – and even in that darkness I squeezed my eyes shut, blotting out unwanted memories that sprang to mind. But I could not blot out the voice – that voice which plagued me whenever I fell ill and was alone in the room, the ghost that haunted me when my defences were gone.

'Why are you dying of shame, Phyllisia?' it asked. 'There are so many other things worth dying of.' Squeezing myself into a tighter ball I tried not to hear the mockery, tried not to answer the silly question, but the voice insisted, 'Tell me, Phyllisia, why are you dying of shame?'

'You know why,' I answered. 'It's because Daddy is such a fraud.'

Voice: 'Tell my why, Phyllisia? Why do you think your father is a fraud?'

I: 'You remember – you must remember when he said, "... I'm running in bad luck ... these picky-headed ragamuffin ..." He meant poor people. And he's making his money off poor people and – and – and drunks.'

Voice: 'You really are talking about Edith, aren't you? But it wasn't your father who said to that poor little girl "... at least she would know I never went barefoot ..."'

I: 'I didn't say it! I only thought it! But I was sorry afterwards. You know I was sorry. If you know so much, you know how sorry I was.'

Voice: 'Were you sorry, Phyllisia? Were you really sorry? Then why didn't you go to her? You knew she needed you.'

I: 'I was afraid! But I would not have been if I knew he was such a fake!'

Voice: 'Why do you keep saying that your father is a fake and a fraud? Has he ever deceived you?'

I: 'Yes! Always! He always deceived me!'

Voice: 'Did you ever try to change him?'

I: 'No!'

Voice: 'But if he always deceived you, you should have tried to change him.'

I, angrily: 'But he's a grown man! How can I change a grown man? After all, I'm only a little girl.'

Voice: 'A little girl? Come now, Phyllisia. You are fifteen, almost sixteen. I was married at seventeen. But of course you would say that was a different time. Let us talk about Edith. How old is Edith?'

I: 'She's my age.'

Voice: 'Yet she is responsible. What about your responsibility, Phyllisia?'

I, almost hysterical: 'Responsible to whom?'

Voice: 'To your poor friend Edith, to Ruby, your father . . .'

I: 'I'm a prisoner in this house! How can a prisoner be responsible to anyone?'

Voice: 'The same way a prisoner can roam through the park every day – plan on making love.'

I: 'You twist everything around. I never know what you are talking about!'

Voice: 'Don't you, Phyllisia? Don't you really? Or do you want to remain blind? But then that's only natural, you are so much like him.'

I: 'That's a lie! I am not like him. I never want to be like him! He is a fake, I tell you. He's a fraud!'

Voice: 'There – you said it again. Think, Phyllisia, think, and then tell me why he is a fake and a fraud.'

I: 'He lies! He doesn't own a big restaurant, with waiters dressed in dark suits waiting on tables! He waits on the counter! And did you know he strips off his fine clothes when he gets into that place? That's what he does, he strips and stands behind the counter shouting and sweating in a polo shirt. Did you know that?'

Voice, laughing: 'And because of that you want to lie down and die? Dear Phyllisia. Dear, dear Phyllisia. But you see, I love you too . . .'

All night I twisted and turned in my sleep, and by the next morning, although I tried desperately to hold on to it, the fever broke. Once again I was fully aware of sounds outside myself. When Ruby dressed and went to the kitchen, I awaited her return, but she took long, very long. When she came back into the room, I was sitting up in bed.

'What were you doing so long in the kitchen?'

'I was fixing Daddy some breakfast.'

'Fixing Daddy's breakfast? Why? Why can't he eat in his restaurant?'

'It just seems to me that he would appreciate one meal a day in his own home, away from that smelly old place. I would fix meals for him every day if only he would let us stay. But he is so set on sending us away. He won't even let me finish the term.'

Silently I studied Ruby as she prepared to leave for school. She was so graceful, so gracious, so nice. Her pretty brown eyes, made to reflect sorrow, seemed more mournful than ever now. 'Ruby,' I said, stopping her at the door. 'Didn't it surprise you?'

'Didn't what surprise me?'

'Daddy's restaurant. Weren't you surprised at how small it was and how filled it was with those – those men . . .'

'Surprised? Why should that surprise me? Didn't Daddy always say that the reason he didn't want us there was because it was too full of men?'

Startled, I lay staring at the door after she had gone. How was it that Ruby saw things so much more differently than I did? Sure Calvin had told us about the place being filled with men, but he had also said that it was a big . . .

Think, Phyllisia, think.

No! He had not. He had only said that one day he would own . . . My mind buzzed, my head ached, thoughts chased each other through my mind.

He had said he was the biggest man in Harlem, and for the biggest man in Harlem to own a place like . . .

No! He had only said he was going to be . . .

But he said he was rich. I heard him . . .

No! He never had. And I should have known. Hadn't I listened to many of his arguments with Mr Charles when he tried to borrow money?

Still he had *implied* all of those things with his big talk and his bragging, or I would never have been so deceived. Yet, why had Ruby seen things so much differently?

Then, just like that, it was clear. I had seen things the way I *wanted* them to be. I had wanted to be the unhappy princess living with the cruel king of a father. I had wanted to be the daughter of the owner of a big restaurant. Perhaps it was because the kids in school had

184

been so hard on me. I didn't know. But I had wanted to be rich, to live in luxury, so that I could feel superior to them – to people like Edith. Calvin had never lied to me. *I* was the fraud.

I shuddered, chilled by my revelation and by the sound of Calvin's footsteps pounding up the hall towards my room. I had too recently been forced to face myself to be able to face him. I pulled my head under the covers. But he pushed open the door and came to stand over the bed.

'I checked your school yesterday. They tell me you don't go. Good. You don't have to go no more. But I'm warning you. Don't leave this house. I don't want you to move until I pack you up bag and baggage and ship you home. If you do, so help me God, you'll find your tail reaching The Island in a coffin!'

I did not answer. Because, as he was speaking, it became clear to me that I *had* to go out. I had to go to Edith. If I understood anything now, it was that I *was* almost sixteen and I had never accepted any responsibility. I had even blamed Calvin for *my* treatment of Edith. But I was the one who had made her suffer. She was *my* friend. I had to go to her.

The moment I heard the door slam, I was out of bed, dressing. I waited a few minutes for fear he might have forgotten something and come back. Stealthily I left the house and hurried up the block. Calvin was not in sight, yet my back crawled with the knowledge that he would double back to the apartment to check on me. It did not matter. I had to go.

A group of men were standing on Edith's stoop blocking the entrance when I arrived. They parted to let me pass without once stopping their conversation. I walked up the rickety, wooden steps, listening for footsteps to follow me; no one did. I remembered the last visit when I stood outside so filled with fear that I might be attacked or raped that I did not enter. Why? No one had bothered me or followed me up these steps in the dozens and dozens of times I had come last summer.

I knocked at Edith's door, not really expecting anyone to answer. The children would be at school and Edith probably at work. But at least I had come. I knocked again, and the second time I was rewarded by the sounds of feet shuffling towards the door. The door cracked open slowly, reluctantly, a face appeared, and I was looking, once again, at my dear friend Edith.

She did not recognize me at first. I suppose she never expected to see me again. Then slowly recognition came. 'Phyl?' she asked. 'Phyl? Is that you?'

'Yes, it's me,' I answered, and she stepped aside to let me enter the familiar room.

Nothing seemed to have changed in that old room. The sink was still stacked with dirty dishes, the old pot-bellied stove still held the big pot on top. Even the chair where the old man had sat at the window seemed never to have been moved; the limp curtain separating the kitchen from the rest of the house was the same. Yet there was a terrible difference: The food on the dishes in the sink had dried and hardened with time, the pot on the stove was fixed in its overflow of dried liquids, and the curtain – agitated by the ghosts of memories of children from behind to embrace me – hung limp and silent. The air of the house was heavy with the staleness of aged food and loud with emptiness.

'The children are in school?' I asked.

'No,' she replied, still looking at me. It was a look without joy, and this I had not expected. But then it was all a part of my dream world that dictated that she loved me more than I her. After all, why should she? How did I deserve it? 'No,' she repeated, 'they're not in school.' Sinking down on the bed-couch, looking wearily around the room as though she too was a stranger, she looked strange to me. It took a while before I realized that it was because she seemed young, fragile, helpless, totally unlike the Edith I had known. 'They got them. They got Bessie and Suzy.'

'They . . .?'

'The city folks. They got them in the orphanage.'

'Oh . . .' Poor Edith. What hadn't she given up and gone through to have *them* win in the end! 'Not Ellen? They didn't take Ellen?'

'Ellen? No, they didn't take her – Ellen is dead, Phyl.'

Ellen dead! How? Why? What had been happening since I had not been to this house? How long had it been? Six, seven months? Ellen was still a baby!

'She's dead, Phyl,' Edith repeated. Her gaze that had been travelling listlessly around the room came to rest on me. Her nostrils flared, hardened, reddened. Tears filled her eyes. 'She's dead, dead, dead, Phyl. And I'm the one to blame.'

Shaking myself from my stunned silence, I rushed to her side, placed my arm around her small, shaking shoulders. 'Don't say things like that, Edith. How can you be to blame?'

Leaning against me she sobbed, big, ugly sobs, filling the ugly room with harsh memories of poverty, of deprivation, of secrecy. And I knew even before Edith explained that Ellen's death had to do with our secret, our terrible secret – and if *she* was in any way to blame, *I* was to blame too. I remembered being even glad that her father had disappeared. I thought he was unimportant then, and didn't really mind taking that vow to keep it a secret.

'It was nothing, Phyl. I swear it was nothing. Just the measles. I taken care of both Suzy and Bessie when they got it. But she got so sick, Phyl. She got so weak and sick. One night she got the fever so bad that her teeth got all baked white. I was so scared that I just picked her up and run all the way to the hospital. But she died. Doctor said it had something to do with malnutrition. Didn't have any resistance, he said. But I fed her, Phyl. You know how good I fed her?'

I nodded, thinking to the mornings with heaped-up plates of hominy grits and fat-back pork grease, of evenings with black-eyed peas and neck bone. 'Yes, you fed her well,' I agreed, 'she always had plenty to eat.'

'I never taken her to a clinic or nothing. But she ain't never been sick.'

'How did they get Bessie and Suzy? Was it because you had to go to the hospital?'

She nodded. 'You know Randy got killed?'

'Yes, I know.'

'It started then. The people kept coming around every day. I wouldn't let the kids answer the door, and they stopped coming. I figgered that anyway they would bury Randy. But, Phyl, I didn't know nothing about getting Ellen buried. She was so little, Phyl. I didn't want them to just open up a hole in the ground and stick her in it. I wanted to bury her decent – so she wouldn't be cold and lonely like Randy – you know what I mean?' I nodded.

'Well, I sent Bessie around to the welfare. Told her to say her mother sent her. But you know those folks. They kept prying, I guess, and Bessie must have told them everything. They kept her and then came around here and got Suzy.'

'How come they didn't take you?'

'I was working. But Bessie and Suzy told them where I was. I guess they wanted me to know what happened to them. I'd have worried. They came and talked to the woman I work for. I wasn't there.'

'Did she tell on you – where you were?'

'No, but the city folks scared her something awful. Said that she would get into all kinds of trouble if she kept me working for her.'

'Then you don't even have a job!'

'Don't matter, I'm going in too.'

'To the orphanage?'

'Yeah. The woman I worked for said that they told her they would put me back in school and teach me a trade until I was eighteen. Said I could look out for the kids while I'm in there and I'll get a job afterwards and take care of them when they come out. So I'm going in. And anyway, what good is it out here without the kids. I don't have nobody else in the world.'

'When will you be going?'

'Today. I called them this morning and they supposed to send somebody after me. I thought it was them when you knocked.'

'But when did all of this happen?'

'It was Sunday when Ellen died. I sent Bessie to the folks Monday. I been hiding out ever since. Just come back last night.' All this had been happening while I had been playing around in the park with José. I shuddered. Would I ever want to see him again after that? I didn't think so.

We sat side by side, waiting for whoever was coming for Edith, holding hands – maybe even thinking the same thoughts. If all the city people said was true, then why had she struggled so hard to keep them out of the orphanage? Why hadn't we found out? Why hadn't I? Why hadn't I been able to talk to Mother – to Calvin? Why hadn't we at least thought of Miss Lass? But thinking of Miss Lass made me shudder again. We could have gone to a policeman. Which one? The one who had killed her brother because he was running? Why hadn't there been some way out of our ignorance? I didn't know. The only thing I did know was that Edith was the only blameless one.

'And what about you, Phyl? Hiya doin'?' She tried to smile. 'You know you're looking good, real good.'

She had said this because she knew how stupidly pleased I always was to get a compliment. That she would even *think* of pleasing me at this time when her world had fallen to pieces around her, made me feel even more deeply my shame.

'Edith, I came here to tell you how badly I feel about not coming to see you – especially after Randy died.' I waited for her answer, but she only shrugged. 'And I came to tell you what a great person I think you are. You're the greatest person that I know. You did a lot for me. A lot for the kids. And you are not to blame for anything – everything you did is because you loved them – and that makes you the most wonderful person to them too . . .'

'You think that, Phyl? You really think that? I used to think that love was everything until Ellen . . .' Tears came again and I cried too.

'I *know* that, Edith. And another thing, Edith. Don't ever say again you don't have anybody. You have me. And you'll have me as long as I live.'

She looked at me a long time, seriously, there was no time left for the little games that children play or dream of – not any more. 'You really mean that, don't you, Phyl?' she said in a sort of wonder. 'You really mean it?'

'Yes, I really mean it, Edith. I do. And wherever they send you, I'm going to come to see you.'

'You will, Phyl? You honest to goodness, really, will?'

'Every week, I swear, Edith.'

But Calvin was sending me away! The thought, sharp and sudden, caused a pain to rip from my stomach to my heart. But I had said it, and I would not unsay it. I had abused her enough. 'And the weeks I can't come I'll write.'

'Swear it?' She raised her right hand.

'I swear.' I raised my right hand too.

23

When I left home, I had known that he would be waiting for me when I returned, belt in one hand, aeroplane ticket in the other. But I had not expected this. He met me at the door, white-lipped with anger. 'Come in and start to pack,' were his first words. 'You think you will play with me like if I'm a mouse. But you wrong. You want to see me in jail – buried. But no! If I touch you. I'll kill you! So I won't put me hands on you. Drive me mad? Never! Just come in and pack your things!'

He led me to my room, and opening the drawers of the dresser, he began to pull things out – mine and Ruby's – and began to pile them on the bed. 'I call and make reservations. Seven o'clock and all you gone. Tonight. The minute your sister get home from school, we start.' He wasn't asking any questions. He did not want to hear anything. He refused to look at me.

How to start talking to a man who was deaf and blind as far as I was concerned? Still, I had to talk to him. We couldn't leave now – today. Not without Edith knowing where I was, I not knowing how to reach her. I had promised her, and I had to keep my promise.

All the way home I had been trying to think of words that would force him to listen to me, words that would make him change his mind about sending us away. If he had asked me where I had been, that would have been an opening. If he had beaten me, I had planned to accept every blow, without crying, and to plead with him afterwards. But he didn't beat me, nor did he ask questions.

Standing in the doorway I watched as he piled the clothes on the bed, higher and higher, cutting off any chance of a compromise. I felt the fragility of my will. What was it I could possibly say to a man I had never really spoken to? Even under the best of circumstances we had hardly exchanged more than two sentences, never a paragraph. How to start now?

He moved around the room in the same blind rage, opening up the closets, taking out our hanging clothes – even our winter things that we would never need. Getting on a chair, he reached into the upper closets for our suitcases which he threw down at my feet. Then he stepped down, panting, and faced me in the doorway saying: 'Now, get to packing!'

He expected me to move, simply get out of his way so that he could pass. But I did not step aside. He looked at me with hard, furious eyes, unrelenting eyes that knew no pity. I still did not move. He either had to ask me to move or had to push me out of his way. But to touch me would be to release his fury, and to ask me would be to acknowledge my will – neither of which he had any intention of doing.

So he simply stood there trying to command me with his anger. I did not cringe, melt or wilt under his gaze, and from the source of my own bravery, words that I had not even prepared, spoke themselves:

'Mother said that I was like you, and now I know what she meant. I don't know you. I never did. And you don't know me. You never tried. Now you are sending

193

us away so that you don't have to know or care who we are and what we think.'

My tone, rather than the words, surprised me as much as it did him. It forced me to keep on talking and him to stand there and listen. 'I don't want to go away,' I said. 'I don't want to go away because I promised my friend that I would come to see her every week while she is in the orphanage.'

'And what that got to do with me?' His anger, which surprise had lessened for a moment, rekindled.

'Her baby sister died because of you!'

'Me!' He put both hands to his chest in astonishment.

'Yes, you. Because I was afraid of you. I couldn't even tell Mother when her father disappeared and she was left alone with her sisters. She saved my life, and I couldn't even tell you. You hated her and called her a ragamuffin. You chased her out of the house, and it didn't matter that she was decent and good, because she was poor. And I let you.' Tears came to my eyes.

He remembered. And it surprised me that he should remember. I knew he remembered by the flash of guilt that broke our stare and made his eyelids quiver. Yet he refused to accept any blame. 'I ain't know what you talking about.' He spoke with lessening anger. 'What I got to do with some girl dying because I run my house the way I want to run it?'

'It's not that,' I cried, my anger mounting. 'I let you chase her out of the house and I was glad because I really believed that I was better than she.'

'Well, you look a damn sight better. I'll tell you that.'

'I didn't know then you made your living off poor people.'

194

'What the hell you talking?' he shouted. 'I ain't make no living off poor people. I make a living off people! And what you talking, you don't know. My life secret? The business there open day and night.'

'I didn't know because I could never talk to you.'

'I still ain't know what you saying.' He looked baffled. 'And anyhow you going some place with somebody you can talk to.'

'That's what I'm trying to tell you, Daddy. I promised Edith. I'm the only one she has in the world to come to see her. She's my friend. I love her.'

'What stupidness. Love? What you do for her with that? If you did love her so much, you would have given her some decent clothes to visit with your mother. Then maybe I wouldn't think she had jinx on she tail and have to chase she out.'

He was hard. I would never have believed that anyone could be so hard. Change? How could I change this man? It would take forever. Yet this was the man that Mother had said she loved and whom Mr Charles and Cousin Frank admired. Even Ruby acted funny about him. I would never understand what made some people love other people.

'Look,' he said, pointing at the clock. 'The plane leave at seven. You can't wait for your sister to come to pack. Start now.' He moved to pass around me, but I stood firm. Knowing I had already lost, there was nothing more to do but try. 'Daddy,' I said in desperation. 'You said you wanted us with you. You said so to Cousin Frank and Mr Charles the other night.'

'I was wrong. I'm a hard-working man. I work night and day to take care of you two. I can't do that and have

195

to worry about where you are and what you doing night and day. New York is a big city, too big to have my worries walking around it.' That's what he was, a hard-working man. Loud, bragging, sometimes brutal, but a hard-working man.

'I was wrong too, Daddy. I've been staying out late because I wanted to spite you. But it was because you were so mean and unreasonable. You said such bad things to Ruby that night. You beat her. And it wasn't true those things you said, Daddy. Not one word of it was true.

'But you wouldn't listen. You *never* listen. And I agree, if we can never talk it's no use us staying here. I want you to know, though, I will never be spiteful again. And Daddy, I – I – I'm much older today than I was yesterday.'

He looked at me strangely. His entire face underwent a change and I knew that for the first time he was regarding me as a person, apart from himself. But then he shook his head. 'I – I – I don't know . . .' He looked at the clock and repeated, 'I – don't know what you talking.'

'And what about Ruby?' I asked.

'What about she?'

'She doesn't want to go either.'

'So, she don't want to go. So what? Look, I make reservations on the seven o'clock plane. I'm not taking even one chance that it might leave late. At seven I want you and your sister and all of my headache on that plane. How you talking? *I* must change *my* plans just like that because you get grown in one night, and because your sister don't want to go. You talking stupidness.'

'Ruby doesn't want to go because she wants to take care of you.'

'Of me?' He put his astonished hands to his chest again. 'But what you think happen to *me* overnight? I ain't still grown? I can't take care of me?'

'You see how you never understand anything that we say to you?' I cried. 'Ruby wants to take care of you because she loves you, Daddy!'

His face quivered at the words, it quivered and quivered, his eyebrows, the muscles of his cheeks twitched and jerked. 'Get out of me way,' he said gruffly, and he pushed me aside.

I stood listening as he walked heavily down the hall to the kitchen, then to his room, then back up the hall, passing me, still standing in the doorway of my room. He went to the living room and I heard him as he walked to the front door and stood. I could feel him waiting, searching his mind for that final command.

'Look,' he finally barked down the hall at me. 'You see all those things you have piled up on that bed. Put them away, nuh? I can't understand it at all, at all. Two grown-up young ladies keeping their room in such a state. I don't want to see it like that again, you hear me? If I see it like that, watch what I do to you tail.' Then he went out slamming the door angrily behind him.

Two books by Rosa Guy in the Puffin Plus series
(for older readers)

EDITH JACKSON

THE DISAPPEARANCE

Heard about the Puffin Club?

... it's a way of finding out more about Puffin
books and authors, of winning prizes (in
competitions), sharing jokes, a secret code, and
perhaps seeing your name in print! When you
join you get a copy of our magazine, *Puffin
Post*, sent to you four times a year, a badge
and a membership book.
For details of subscription and an application
form, send a stamped addressed envelope to:

The Puffin Club Dept A
Penguin Books Limited
Bath Road
Harmondsworth
Middlesex UB7 0DA

and if you live in Australia, please write to:

The Australian Puffin Club
Penguin Books Australia Limited
P.O. Box 257
Ringwood
Victoria 3134